I0823345

SODA LAKE

SODA LAKE

A NOVEL

JOHN C HAMPSEY

RARE BIRD
LOS ANGELES, CALIF.

THIS IS A GENUINE RARE BIRD BOOK

Rare Bird Books
6044 North Figueroa Street
Los Angeles, California 90042
rarebirdbooks.com

FIRST HARDCOVER EDITION, OCTOBER 2025

For more information, address:
Rare Bird Books Subsidiary Rights Department
6044 North Figueroa Street
Los Angeles, California 90042

Cover painting by Armando Marino
Author photograph by Eric Johnson

Set in Adobe Garamond
Printed in the United States

10 9 8 7 6 5 4 3 2 1

Library of Congress Cataloging-in-Publication Data available upon request

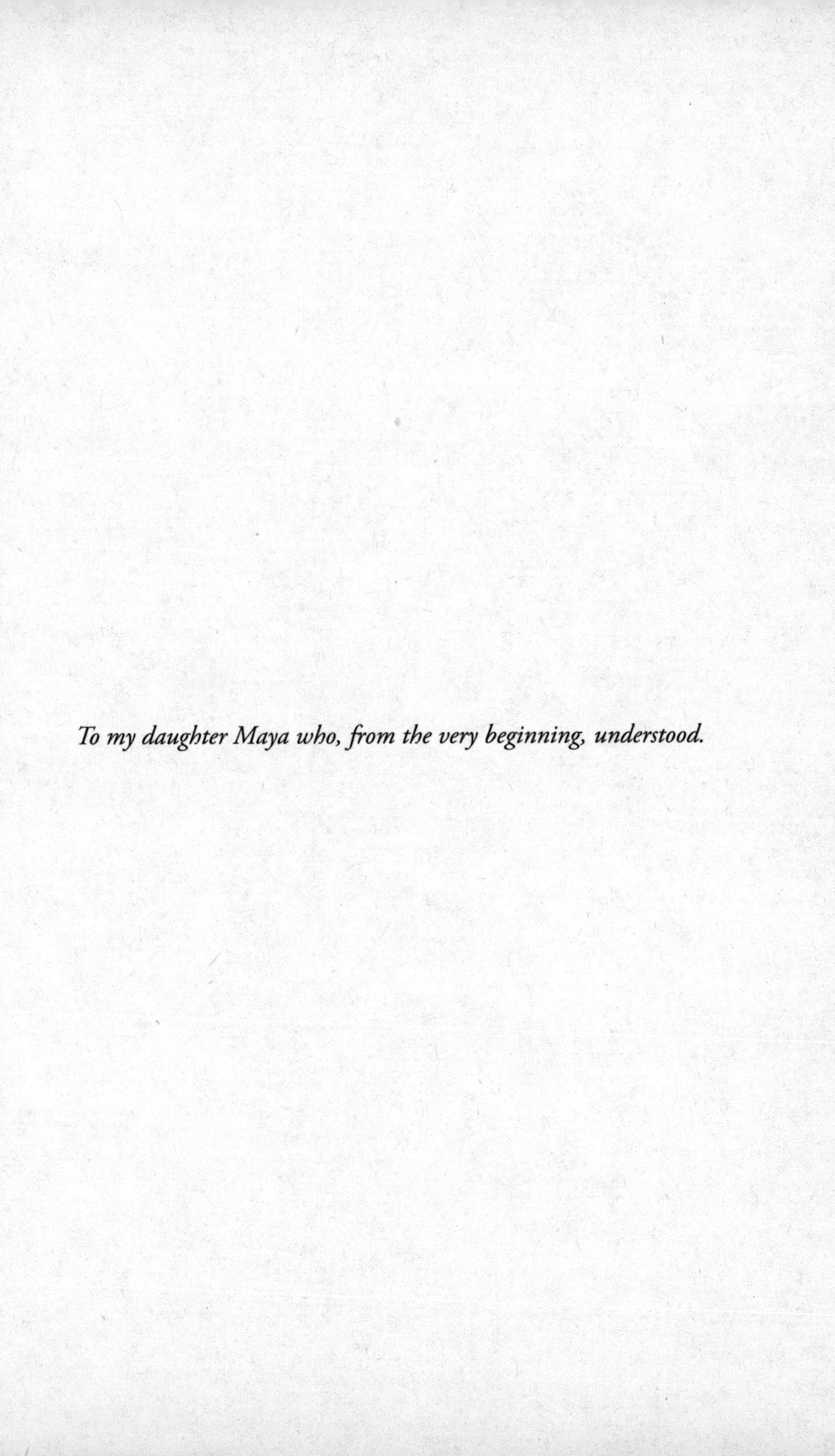

To my daughter Maya who, from the very beginning, understood.

CONTENTS

Chapter One
SODA LAKE

I never knew about Soda Lake until I was driving south on Route 58 into the Carrizo Plain one Saturday afternoon…on my way to Painted Rock. I was going to a friend's wedding and was already late, so I was concentrating on the road and didn't see Soda Lake until it was there—expansive, white, shimmering…and nearly unreal in the purple sunlight.

A sign said Scenic Overlook. So I turned right and drove up the hill, parked in a small field, and climbed a path through the dry, hot air until I could look over the Carrizo Plain and the white salt lake stretching into the horizon.

Below, an automobile pulled over and a man in dark clothes jumped out and started running across the lake. The car drove away and the man continued running like someone was chasing him. But there was no one else around.

Maybe he just wants to run across a lake. And Soda Lake is the only place he can do that.

After a few moments, the man's pace slowed, as if his legs were caught in netting. *It's the lake crust. He's collapsing through the shelves into the soda dust below.*

Eventually he fell forward and crawled on his knees. He got harder to see, the white lake absorbing him into a glint of sunlight.

At one point his wavering image seemed to reappear, before frittering away into the bleached air. I squinted; waited for him to appear again. When he didn't, I drove down the hill and parked next to the lake.

I couldn't see him when I got out of the car, but his footprints were still visible in the lake. So I stepped into them, my feet dropping deeper the farther I went. Still, I couldn't see the man. He was blending into the white abyss, even with his dark clothes.

Yoo-hoo! I yelled. Anyone out there?

There was nothing back.

If I didn't leave soon, I would miss the wedding and my friend, with flowers around her waist, parading in widening circles through the California chaparral.

I returned to shore in the same footprints, my shoes sinking into a primordial black muck that cloyed at my feet, making it harder to lift my legs.

After reaching the car, I removed my shoes and drove another fifteen miles down Soda Lake Road…into the thickening late-afternoon sunlight.

There weren't any cars in the parking lot at Painted Rock and the gate was closed. *Maybe the wedding is over…and she will think I was late on purpose. And if I told her about a man disappearing into Soda Lake, she wouldn't believe me…*

The wind had almost ceased, like it always does just before sunset.

I sensed her presence around me…wistful, moonfaced, quietly smiling…

Atop the hill, Painted Rock seemed daunting, solid…an unflinching presence amidst the soft undulations of the orange-tinted chaparral.

Famous for its ancient Chumash Indian pictographs, the rock structure is horseshoe shaped. It looks like a giant vagina, she liked to say. And that's why she wanted to get married there…before the deadline when all public ceremonies at Painted Rock would cease, in order to preserve the site and the iconography sacred to the Chumash.

Her marriage there would be the last.

At the head of the trail to Painted Rock was a sign warning of rattlers. Next to it, an unwrapped cigar, which I put in my pocket. In the dead brown grass to my right was a string of black-eyed daisies. *Probably from the wedding.* When I picked them up, the flowers disintegrated in my hand.

The static air was filled with gnats, and the sweat started coming on…with it, a feeling of hopelessness—I wouldn't make it to Painted Rock and back before dark.

I wanted to rest, but there was nowhere to sit away from the gnats, and the ticks hiding in the tall grass, and the snakes.

Wouldn't it be better to return to Soda Lake and check on the man in dark clothes. Because who can see Indian drawings in the dark anyway?

A half hour later, I was parked again next to Soda Lake, which still looked chalky-white below the descending darkness, as if the moon was shining on it. But there was no moon.

I couldn't find the man's footprints in the dim light. So I yelled again. But there was nothing….

Maybe he is dead. And I can't call the police because they will think I made it all up. And if they did believe me, they might find my footprints inside his, which wouldn't be good either.

Disappointed that I had missed the wedding and lost the dark-clothed man, I couldn't face going home.

I drove north on the winding and precarious Pozo Road and, after edging a few miles through the blackness, stopped at an old wooden hotel next to a closed down general store in the remote town of La Panza. There were no other buildings around.

The hotel clerk was young, thin-faced, with long sideburns. He said he didn't have any rooms available, but for twenty dollars I could sleep on a couch on the upstairs porch. I climbed the stairs before he changed his mind.

From my perch, I kept watch on the road below…trying to ignore my hunger.

If I drive to Pozo for dinner, I might find someone else sleeping on the couch when I return.

Not a single car drove by and the hotel was quiet, making me wonder if the clerk had lied and there really were vacant rooms.

Before dawn, I heard someone running up and down the stairs. Then it was quiet again, except for a dog howling in the distance.

In the morning, a pile of shiny, hard bagels waited in a turquoise bowl on the front desk. They looked like something that should not be eaten, but perhaps hung on the wall as ornamental art.

I asked for cream cheese and the same clerk from the night before said in staccato—No cream cheese, only bagels, like he was pretending to be Chinese.

He disappeared behind a door, and I grabbed two bagels to make up for the missing cream cheese and started eating one as I drove back down the canyon road toward Soda Lake. The bagel was dry and hard to swallow, and I wished I had some coffee. But once you leave La Panza and head into the California Valley, there is nowhere to stop. So I threw the bagels out the window for the birds.

At Soda Lake, I parked at the exact spot where the man had run from the car. But I didn't see his footprints anymore. *They couldn't have washed away because it hadn't rained. And if someone covered them up, I would see shovel marks.*

I really did see him, I reminded myself. *I found his footprints and walked inside them. Maybe I didn't go out far enough....*

I walked onto Soda Lake and didn't break through the crust because the soda dust had turned into hot ice. There would be no footprints to leave behind.

My march continued on top of Soda Lake, like a miracle.

Who can do this? Only a god.

In a courageous moment I turned around...my car looked far away in the morning haze. I paused, trying to remember if I had locked the car doors. And then it didn't matter because I could no longer see the car.

Maybe I should just go home. Because the temperature is rising, and I have no water.

Some black crows flew overhead on their way to find my bagels at the side of the road.

I took a few more steps into Soda Lake and then stopped.

Suddenly overcome with exhaustion, I considered crawling instead.

Chapter Two

THE GARAGE WALL MAN

I

When I entered the garage room, I realized I had forgotten to throw the chicken dung out in the morning. It lay there, dry and ancient-looking, on a leaf of newspaper atop the washing machine.

I carried it through the heavy wooden gate, across the driveway, and up the three stairs to the gray bin underneath the orange trees at the side of the garage. After closing the crusty lid, I thought I heard a cough coming from the garage wall, even though it didn't make any sense. I stared into the darkness, straining to see from the streetlight filtering through the leaves of the trees. But there was nothing.

As I reached the stairs, some of the gravel shifted behind me. I looked back and stopped breathing to listen, waiting for my eyes to adjust to the dim light. Gradually, a darker shape grew out of the shadows—the rough outline of a man lying against the bottom of the garage wall.

Shit, a voice said, with the tone of someone who has been caught.

A car passed up the hill, the headlights flashing through the trees and I saw him distinctly for a moment—his face astonishingly clean-shaven, his body lounging like someone at a swimming pool. His right hand was cocked behind his head and his legs crossed.

He must be from the drug house on the other side of the hill. They always have vagabonds coming and going, and the police don't care. But he doesn't look like—

You don't have a problem with me sleeping here? he asked, his voice calm.

What?

I know your patterns. I'm never in your way. But then this damn cough.

He coughed again, as if to prove it to himself, and to me.

When you dump your ashtray in the garbage every night, you never see me.

He shifted his position, his body shuffling some dead brittle leaves. Even in the dimness, I could see he was lying on something, a piece of cardboard maybe. I backed a few steps toward the driveway, in case he decided to stand up.

I'm still lying on the ground, he said. You don't have to worry.

You can't sleep there, mister.

What do you care, you're living alone now, he said, gesturing with his left hand in the air.

My daughter lives with me! And—

You can go on as you always do. Forget you ever saw me…and everything will be like it was.

He spoke as if he hadn't heard me or hadn't listened. And I wished I could see him better.

Don't worry, I'm not going to make soup out of your precious chickens. Though I do take an egg every now and then. Eat it right out of the shell with a little straw, pure protein. A man can live on just one egg. And I get rid of the shell, so you don't have to worry about that. I've never taken anything else.

You can stay there tonight. But when I come out tomorrow night you have to be gone, or I'll call the police.

Your daughter doesn't take care of the chickens as much as she used to…. What happened?

When I didn't answer, the garage wall man dropped his head back on his shoulder, as if he had nothing else to say. But as I moved down the steps to the driveway, he began talking again, something about always taking the cardboard with him in the morning so I didn't have to worry about that either. I wasn't sure if he was talking to himself or to me.

Back in the garage room, I poured myself a brandy and walked over to the wall and listened to see if I could hear him still talking on the other side. But there was only a ticking sound in the roof that was probably the termites.

I put an old Van Morrison record on the one-piece stereo I inherited when my mother died, hoping the music would distract me from the garage wall man. But the needle was worn and the speakers sounded tinny, and my chance at escape didn't happen. So I lit a cigarette and looked over some manuscript notes spread atop the washing machine. It was no use, though, the garage wall man had ruined everything.

I considered going back to the wall to see if there was a crack I could see through, then I could watch him without him knowing it. But the cracks are always on the outside where the stucco crumbles. That's why nothing inside ever gets out. And why there is never enough room where we already are…making me wish I could see in the dark, like the animals.

But we live within our own private bodies, even when the other side is just six inches of plaster away, where the garage wall man sleeps on his cardboard bed trying not to think about the next day…when a dog will cross the street to fight with another dog for a reason only dogs understand, and passing cars with drivers whom the garage wall man imagines must be happy…while the puffy white air circulates on its own, pressing against the membrane of the sky until something gathers to begin, no matter the time, because nothing really depends on that…for a garage wall man who only sees in black and white.

At me, too, someone watches and wonders. I have seen them from the perch in my study, walking by the house, always gazing upward…and the cars traveling fast up the hill because the people inside are unhappy…and late-night students stumbling and blathering about something they think they understand, then hollering louder because they understand it again.

I turned off the record player and left my unfinished brandy on top of the dryer. After switching off the light, I went inside the house even though I was anxious to know if the garage wall man was still there. I desired to hear him again and considered returning to the garage and pinning my ear up against the wall. But I shut off the living room lamp and went down to bed.

The next night, I avoided dumping the ashtray into the gray bin because I didn't want to know if the garage wall man was there… lounging against the wall, waiting for me. So I emptied the ashtray over the fence instead, hoping the neighbors wouldn't notice.

After lighting a cigarette and pouring a brandy, though, I felt drawn to the side of the garage because I told him I would call the police, and I didn't want him to think I was the kind of man who wouldn't do what he said.

Everything was just as it was the night before, only this time I had a flashlight.

Where's your ashtray? he asked.

I aimed the flashlight near his feet, but could still see his clean-shaven cheeks, and I wanted to ask how he managed that if he had no place to live.

So, are you going to call the police?

His face was handsome, strong-looking. He could have been a neighbor who just happened to be lying beneath my orange trees at night. He wore a dark coat that went almost to his feet and brown worker boots that appeared new. His right hand was poised upon his hip.

You don't think I will make the call?

I don't care if you do. I'll be gone by the time they get here, and back after they leave. And if you call a second time, they won't believe you. Besides, you're not the kind of person who wants the police coming to your house.

He was right, but I didn't want to admit it.

You don't know me, because no one really—

I know your wife is gone. Traveling, is she? It's been months now, so I guess—

Have you been going through my mail? Because if you've done that, then—

Not that long ago, I lived in Paris, he said, changing the subject. I met a man named McCuade, from Donegal, Ireland. Have you been to Donegal?

I've been to Ireland.

Of course. Well, McCuade, he's the only man in my life that I...believe was worthy of love.

He paused....

Something timeless...between McCuade and me. I'm telling you, even though you probably can't understand.

I didn't want to hover over him anymore, so I sat on the low wall next to the orange trees and turned off my flashlight. A moment later, he pulled something from his coat pocket.

Since you're sitting, you don't mind if I smoke the last part of this cigar, do you? I never get to smoke out here because it would draw attention. But now...why don't you go get your brandy and cigarettes?

That's okay. I'm fine.

I wanted to get my brandy and cigarettes, but he would want a brandy, too, and then—

I'm Irish as well, he said, raising his voice just a bit, like he was excited to talk whether I listened or not, his words smooth and steady, not like a homeless person rattling on.

Two generations back, my family came from a small town outside Belfast.... But McCuade, he's from the kidneys of Ireland—northern Donegal!

I know you're Irish, he continued, looking up from his cigar. But do you actually know what county your great grandfather came from?

My family is from Cookstown, just west of Belfast.

Ah, well.... But McCuade, he...we ended up in California. At a ranch not far from here. Because I had an old friend who needed his place taken care of. Hot as splayed skin in that valley...and I didn't know anything about ranching. But McCuade did. He could handle those cattle, and he learned to wrestle with the llamas.

So, you and this man, McCuade, came all the way from Paris to run a ranch in central California?

He took a puff from his cigar, the smoke floating into the high shadows of the trees, the orange glow momentarily illuminating his fine clean fingers. He seemed familiar in that moment. Perhaps I had seen him downtown where they panhandle, even though the garage wall man wouldn't do that. Perhaps I had seen him other places as well.

We were out of money in Paris and couldn't pay the bill for our little room on the top floor on Rue Mouffetard. And we had this opportunity…in a letter waiting for me at the American Express. As I said, McCuade knew all about—

What happened?

There was not much left of his cigar, but he seemed intent on smoking it till the end. He touched the ash onto one of the paving stones next to his cardboard bed. I reconsidered getting my brandy and cigarettes, but I didn't want the garage wall man to think we were camping together.

It went well until last fall…. My friend, who owned the ranch, stopped paying the bills. But McCuade kept taking care of the cattle and llamas. He knew each one by name…. A man from the bank showed up one day and told us the ranch was foreclosed, and we had no legal right to be there. Still, we stayed on. We had nowhere else to go. McCuade loved that land and didn't mind the heat. I remember one night after dinner, in the hot stillness, sitting on the porch with Irish whiskeys, he, in his Donegal accent—'We're still ranchers, aren't we, laddy? Like gods we are…living in this valley. Gods with balls of kerosene, lighting up the lifeless land, and the animals beneath us. Beating back the nerves of the sky until everything appears infinite.' In the morning, having coffee on the fog-shrouded porch, eating a cantaloupe we borrowed from a neighbor's field, sharing slices from my knife. McCuade's half smile, jaw jutting. My god, I loved the look of him. I punched a man at the Cayucos Tavern one time, just for bumping into him. McCuade sitting at the center of the bar that could have been the center of the world…smiling, clean-shaven, drinking his black and tan. They threw both of us out of the Tavern. But every now and then, McCuade and I would go back, when we still had the ranch truck to drive, just so they could throw us out again. McCuade loved the playful fury of it. Sometimes we drank so hard we'd forget the truck and walk back to the ranch in the late dark, when so many sounds in the earthly night seem hopeful… A couple months ago, the sheriff came by with one of his deputies and put a sign up in the yard and tape across the front door. Told us we had to leave with him. So we rode with the sheriff alongside a shimmering white expanse. At a bend in the road, McCuade leaned over and told me he couldn't go to the police station because he had no visa. The next moment he jumped out and was running across the lake. The sheriff stopped the car, but didn't pursue him. And McCuade vanished into the dry white lake and sky, just like a god....

Soda Lake?

Do you know it?

What happened after that?

I believe he's back in Donegal. He always told me—"If there's ever any trouble, laddy, I'll just go home." And that's where I'm going, as soon as I can figure a way. McCuade is waiting in Dungloe.

The garage wall man's voice drifted off and his head dropped into the shadows below the line of dappled street light. His cigar was out, his hand fallen to the side. A few seconds later, his body shifted positions on the cardboard and everything went still.

I stood up.

I'm going now. Do you want a blanket?

I don't want anything from you, he said in a low voice, sounding like a different person, remote and lost.

As I headed down the pavers, he spoke again, incantation-like—

You have to keep living through the sudden black blood of things, laddy...because the earth is never quiet. Not nearly quiet enough...with piercing wings fighting the descent. But oh, not madness yet.... And I will punch any damned son of a bitch right into the corner while everyone else is dancing. Until the nerves of the sky are beaten flat and there is a pulse of peace.

II

I didn't bother going into the garage room the following night, but went directly to the side where the garage wall man was already asleep, his body angled and his head facing the stucco wall.

After turning off my flashlight, I sat on the orange tree wall. He seemed to have no sense I was there.

My chain-smoking asthmatic neighbor coughed from across the street. He didn't have a job and spent most of his days and nights smoking, staring out the window, and coughing. I worried about him seeing me beneath the orange trees. I didn't want anyone to know about the garage wall man, so I spoke in a whisper—

Mister, are you awake? Mister? I wanted to let you know, I will find McCuade for you. I'm going to Greece for sabbatical research, but I can stop in Ireland along the way. I've always wanted to go to Donegal. So I can look for McCuade. You just need to give me more information. His full name? Relatives' names?

I don't know why you're talking about McCuade, the garage wall man said without turning his head. I barely remember him. I'll be gone in the morning. I'll take my cardboard with me, and it will be like I was never here. And I won't use your damn water anymore, drinking through the hose like a child…the pressure so slight you never heard the water moving through the house pipes.

But you talked about McCuade last night. Don't you remember?

Forget McCuade, he said, raising his voice.

In the dim light I could see he was unshaven.

What's the matter with you? I asked, struggling to still whisper. Do you want me to bring you something to eat? A sandwich or—

McCuade doesn't exist. I made him up.

I leaned back in disbelief, my hands landing in some sharp needles fallen from the orange trees. How could McCuade not be real, when so much was already depending on him? So much that the garage wall man himself seemed to fade back into the tree shadows until I almost couldn't see him anymore. I was afraid if I turned on my flashlight, he would be nothing but a pile of old wood in the shape of a man.

Feeling my nerves rising, I decided to talk on—

After Ireland, I'm going to Athens, then to Sicyon on the Gulf of Corinth, where Praxilla was from…and on to the island of Paros, because Archilochus was from there. Then to Ephesus, on the coast of Turkey, because that's where Heraclitus, the ancient philosopher, was born. Heraclitus, so arrogant and obnoxious…they threw stones at him during the Olympiad in 504 BC. I want to see what Heraclitus saw…how nothing abides, everything forever becoming. I knew a woman, an anthropologist in Boston, who studied the Samoans, and she said they were the essence of unchanging being. For thousands of years…. And Heraclitus? He fritters away onto his island.

The garage wall man lunged into a sitting position. I could feel him staring, breathing…I could hear his heart.

The rest of us, I continued, we're not like that. We're consumed by fires…something else and something else…. Dreaming of that single filament. While our minds—a swarm of bees. Like, I wanted to be a priest one time, and my mother said you don't have to do that, not for me…. But it wasn't for my mother. I just wanted to live inside the filament. So you would be doing me a favor, mister…if you'd let me try and find McCuade for you.

Worry about yourself and your daughter, he said from the wall shadow before falling back onto his side.

Don't worry, mister, I will always see my daughter. Even in my dream, she is there…just ahead of me…through a window, below in the courtyard, and I am about to descend the stairs. Do you want me to bring you a blanket? Because what does it matter anymore…. Or you could sleep inside the garage. I can put a cot up in the little room. And I won't bother you. I'll stay in the house.

He didn't answer.

I could bring you a cigar, too. I have one from a wedding I went to, out by Soda Lake. You remember Soda Lake, mister. And some matches....

I don't smoke, he snapped, with disdain.

But the night before?

Both of our voices ceased by their own volition. And the garage wall man returned into his shadow. Maybe that is how I missed him for so long, when I headed out to the garbage bin at night.... And he was always there.

III

I couldn't wait for darkness to come the next evening, so I could tell him I was sorry...about everything. I went out earlier than usual, taking with me the brandy bottle and two glasses, the ashtray, cigarettes, and matches, and the cigar from the wedding. I expected him to be clean-shaven and up for talking.

As soon as I turned the corner, I saw him curled on his side, already asleep. I moved quickly up the stairs, tripping on the last step. After I caught my balance, I realized the garage wall man wasn't there at all. It was just a pile of wood inside the shadow. He must have placed the wood there so I would think it was him. And he wasn't worried about termites, because the wood was directly against the wall.

I moved the wood over to the kindling pile, sat on the low wall under the orange trees, and waited...with the absurd bottle of brandy, glasses, and ashtray by my side. Eventually, my back got sore and I went in, taking everything with me except the cigar.

The following morning, when I tossed the chicken dung into the bin, the cigar was still there, but in a different spot farther along the wall. Maybe he had picked it up and decided against smoking it. Unless the wind had rolled it down the pavers. Or maybe a blue jay, or a possum's tail....

Inside the garbage can was a blue sheet of paper that didn't come from my house. It had light pencil scribblings across it at different angles. *A result of writing in the dark.* And the script was slanted the way only a left-handed person would write, making me remember how the garage wall man raised his left hand whenever he gestured, his fingernails shining in the dim light.

I brought the paper inside and looked at it under a lamp. The scribbled words were nearly impossible to decipher. But I copied what I could, stitching them together in a way the Garage Wall Man would have intended.

. . . Tomorrow, flying out of the dark earth, the sudden blood thickens, because I tossed the rock bird, and everything gathered to begin.

Chapter Three
FATHER FENTON

It was Father Fenton's Friday, all along the streets of the town and beyond the big box stores and into the valley fields beneath the brown hills. On Friday he could do anything. He had the car all day to make his rounds, like an old-time doctor would, or like a priest might still do if he was willing to give up his free time for just one day.

His first stop was the Wineman Hotel where lots of old men lived, but Rostrum was the one Father Fenton came to know best because he played his violin most days in front of the ice cream shop on Higuera Street, wearing his bow tie, vest, and heavy brown shoes. People gave him money that he used for fresh fruit or a pair of socks or a haircut. But Rostrum would have played for free. Short and frail, Rostrum was still strong on the strings, stronger it seemed since his wife died two years ago because now he was playing his violin for her.

When Father Fenton walked in, Rostrum's diminutive body was deep inside a large soft chair in the lobby. A brown paper bag rested on his lap; his violin case was on the floor by his feet. His pointed beard was neatly trimmed and his thin tanned hands, with salient blue veins crossing toward the wrists, were poised delicately on his knees. The bag, Father Fenton knew, was filled with fruit, which was all Rostrum would eat until dinner.

Father Fenton paused longer than usual to look at him. And Rostrum eventually smiled back, then looked away toward the windows facing the street.

Are you okay, Rostrum? You look tired.

I always do on Friday, Father, which is the only day you see me.

How are you feeling?

Fine. I'm just resting a bit before I go out.

Have you eaten? Because we have time. I could take you across the street to Louisa's for breakfast. After putting a few more quarters in the meter, we could just walk right over there and—

No, Father, I don't need that. I have my fruit.

He lifted the brown bag into the air to show him.

At the end of the day, Father Fenton knew the meals-on-wheels ladies would deliver dinner to Rostrum and the other men at the Wineman.

Just give me your blessing, Father, and I'll be off.

You're not going to play for me today? Something before…

I'm not ready yet, Father. I need to walk a bit.

Of course, that's fine. I will just bless you now to keep you strong and in God's hands all day.

Rostrum usually kneeled, but not this time. He was too tired.

That's okay, Rostrum. No need to get up.

Father Fenton moved his hand in a studied pattern above Rostrum's head, and Rostrum only half heard the words—Benedictio Dei omnipotentis, Patris et Filii et Spiritus Sancti….

There, my blessing is with you. God's blessing.

Father Fenton felt an urge to touch Rostrum, on his Irish cap maybe or on his smooth cheek just above the beard. But Rostrum wasn't the kind of man you could touch easily, even if you were a priest. And Father Fenton could always tell who he could touch and who he couldn't. Still, he wanted to touch Rostrum because it made the God-flesh connection certain, which is why touching occurred in some form in all of the Catholic sacraments.

Outside in the strong sunshine, Father Fenton felt tired and a little depressed, something he rarely experienced on a Friday when he was making his rounds. A sense of doubt flashed through him—*maybe I'm not really doing any good…maybe I should just stay home on Fridays…. Coffee could bring reinforcements, though. And the uncertainties might fade away….*

At Linnaea's Cafe, Father Fenton filled his cup and walked past the abstract paintings for sale on the wall and into the back courtyard where people could smoke. It didn't bother Father Fenton, who sometimes enjoyed a cigarette himself late at night, in secret.

He settled in at his usual table under the bougainvillea hoping someone might see him there in his collar and believe he was a good man and maybe talk to him as in the old days when no one worried about priests. When they said hello, Father, and meant it.

He sat up straight in his chair, fighting the curved spine problem that afflicted his sisters and brothers, all of them getting it from their father who got it from his father. He tried to read the paper but worried people might think he was too busy for them to say hello. If he didn't read, what would he be seeming to do? Was the priest waiting for someone?

But it was Father Fenton's Friday, not theirs. And he should be able to go anywhere, just like them.

He worried, too, about drinking too much coffee. Because he might have to use the bathroom and there was only one bathroom at Linnaea's. And if he was in there a long time, they might wonder what he was doing. And stare at him when he came out.

So he drank only half a cup, and slowly.

More coffee, Father Fenton? a girl's voice asked.

Why is she asking me if the place is self-service, he wondered. *Is it because of my collar?*

Excuse me…how did you know my name?

That guy over there with the laptop told me. He said you come here most Fridays.

Father Fenton looked toward the young man whose eyes were fixed on his computer screen. He didn't recognize him.

No more coffee. Thank you. And it's pronounced Father *Fentaung*, like the French.

Sure, Father. Have a good day.

She didn't mean that. They never do.

The computer man was tall and rangy, with a slight beard and disturbed hair. Father Fenton wondered what he was looking at on his screen. So he decided to try and see as he passed by to leave. But the young man's eyes tracked onto Father Fenton's eyes, and it was impossible to see anything else.

As he neared the door, Father Fenton wished he had said something. But it was too late. The man with the laptop was three tables behind and Father Fenton was already waving goodbye to the girl at the counter and heading out the door.

At Charles Shoes, Father Fenton actually considered trying something on, like many times before. He rarely bought new shoes, and if he did, they ended up looking the same as his old shoes. Yet he waited, as always, for his friend Jerry to come up and say, Do you see anything you like, Father?

Father Fenton wasn't there for shoes; he was there to see Jerry and to try and get Jerry to go to Mass again. But every time, shoes came into it. Even when Jerry talked to him about his most recent medical procedure, Father Fenton was thinking *shoes,* while staring at Jerry's hair that was more yellow than gray, and the skeletal shape of his cheeks pressing through his thin blue skin, and his large watery eyes that Jerry wiped with his handkerchief…wondering all the while if it really was that important for Jerry to go to Mass, which he had not done since his wife died seven years ago.

On some future Friday, Father Fenton knew Jerry wouldn't be there, and he would wander around the store like he was looking at shoes for the first time. And if someone walked in, he would just be Father Fenton staring at shoes, trying some on, piling up the empty boxes with the white tissue spilling about. And if he did finally buy shoes, paying cash, Jerry wouldn't get the commission. He wanted to warn Jerry about that, but no man can tell another man that, not even a priest.

Would you like to try anything on, Father? Jerry asked from behind.

Not today, Jerry. Maybe next time…I was looking at those tan Clarks, though. But they are slip-ons and would never fit my thin feet.

We could try insoles, Father.

Yes. I know.

More than his skinny feet, Father Fenton worried about his hammer toe that would eventually protrude into the soft leather of any slip-on, until people would notice and think, My gosh, Father Fenton has a bunion! Which is why Father Fenton never wore sandals except with socks.

It was his mother's fault for passing the hammer toe onto him. People never think about those things when they have children. And if someone were to complain about something like that in confession, Father Fenton would say, It is God's way of testing us, to see if we can love our imperfections.

Still, Father Fenton would love to wear slip-ons, especially with the stylish pointed toes. They might not look right on just any priest, but perhaps on a Jesuit....

Can I use your bathroom, Jerry?

Of course, Father. You know where it is. Past the stockroom, on the right. The switch is on the outside.

No one would wonder why he is in there, like at Linnaea's Cafe. But it isn't very clean either, because they didn't have to worry about the public using it, only priests. Father Fenton hoped no hairs were on the rim after he raised the seat, using toilet paper between his fingers. He didn't want to stare at the brown crust around the sink drain either, while standing, waiting.... *If only it could just be Jerry's bathroom, rather than for all the people working there, none of them taking care of anything except shoes.*

After zipping his trousers, Father Fenton avoided the mirror for fear the floating image might not match his idea of who he was. So he focused on his collar—adjusting it and tightening it in back. He washed his hands with soap and no water and wiped them on the back of his pants.

Father Fenton checked his watch as he headed back into the showroom. It was half past one! He must stay on schedule. Get some lunch and head to the valley fields for Mass at 4:00 p.m.

I have to go, Jerry. I'll try something on next week.

Always good to see you, Father.

Next Friday, I'll definitely buy those Clarks. If you think they'd look good on me.

Of course. You can wear anything you want, Father.

Take care of your health now, Jerry. And I'm going to get you to Mass one of these days.

Jerry nodded, but Father Fenton couldn't tell if he was saying yes, or if his head was just shaking from his Parkinson's.

At a red light near the south end of town, Father Fenton saw her heading in his direction from the bridge that crossed the creek. *She must not see me. Not on a Friday.*

Within seconds she would be passing in front of his car. So Father Fenton turned to his right, like he was reaching for something in the back seat. If the light turned green, he hoped the cars behind wouldn't toot their horns because then she would certainly look and recognize him.

But the tooting began. *Don't they see my collar?* Father Fenton wondered.

Yet who can see a priest's collar through two car windows?

He pressed the gas pedal lightly even though he hadn't turned back around, and the car moved slowly with Father Fenton still staring to his right, as if he was waiting for the face of God to appear in the passenger window.

The horns stopped. But Father Fenton didn't trust the quiet, and didn't turn back around. He could use his peripheral to drive. *Because no one gives peripheral vision enough credit...*remembering an old man he used to visit at the nursing home on Fridays who had degenerative eye disease and cocked his head sideways the whole time, and he could see everything.

Father Fenton drove over the bridge, across a creek that ran ten miles to Avila Beach. He tried to imagine himself there, on such a dazzling day of white sun with the fog bank far from shore so he would feel warm on the gray sand. But a priest alone on a beach without his collar is vulnerable...his embarrassing white skin, his skinny legs, and everyone wondering what he was doing there. Was he really just reading a book?

In front of Costco, Father Fenton tried to find a spot in the shade, but the trees in the parking lot were too small to provide any.

Mae was not in her usual place, greeting shoppers with Welcome to Costco! He looked around, getting nervous that he might not find her, and his Friday would spiral into failure.

He decided to check inside the store, but one of the greeters stopped him because he didn't have a Costco card. Mae would have let him in—*Do you think Costco would stop a priest, Father? You go on inside.*

I'm Father Fenton, he said to the greeter. I'm looking for someone who works here. Mae. Do you know her?

She's over there, Father. On her break.

Father Fenton was relieved to see Mae sitting at one of the wind-blown, little plastic tables, but not relieved to see her eating a couple of hot dogs and a large slab of pizza. He waved to her and she waved back, but he decided to get some food for himself before sitting down. At the window, he ordered a sausage dog for only a dollar fifty, and they automatically gave him a bottomless soda cup. He planned on having just water and then maybe sneaking a little Sprite into his cup, but the price was the same whether he got the bottomless soda or not. *No wonder so many like to eat outside at Costco, even though it's in a wind tunnel.*

As he sat next to Mae, a sadness set in that Father Fenton fully expected. *Why is this woman, with such a beautiful face, hundreds of pounds overweight?* He wanted to see past her body, but he knew she would just follow the hotdogs and pizza with a cupcake and more of her eternal soda.

Even as a priest, Father Fenton had no right to say anything. He remembered how miserable he had been as a boy.... So thin the nuns called him Mr. Skinny. And his mother telling him that when he was older, he would be glad to be tall and thin because the most handsome men are always tall and thin. But he didn't believe her. Because his mother's brothers, who were all tall and thin, were terribly stooped and looked old for their age with red faces and trembling red hands. They were never the same after the war, she said one time. And seeing a fat person back then was an oddity—Don't stare, his mother would say.

So Father Fenton felt lucky he could eat whatever he wanted and not worry. Even though, there is no such thing as luck, his mother said. You work hard to get everything you have. *Even my body?* he wondered.

So, how are you today, Mae? I looked for you at the greeting area. But I'm later than usual.

Fine, Father. We just have to take our breaks when it works out for someone else to take our place.

She smiled as he took a bite of his sausage dog and looked around at the people rolling by, their carts stacked high with bulk foods. They, too, were depressing to Father Fenton. And he had no way to reach them. Only Mae, because months ago he found a way to talk to her on Fridays.

Next week, Mae, we could go to lunch somewhere else. What do you think?

Eating here is fine, Father, she said.

I mean somewhere healthier, you know…

I only have thirty minutes, Father. You could bring a lunch for yourself.

Yes, I suppose I could.

Mae finished her hot dogs and moved the pizza slice in front of her. Father Fenton looked toward the parking lot because he didn't want to watch her eat. But he could still catch her face through his peripheral. And she could see him, too, from beyond her high round cheeks.

Father Fenton took another bite of his sausage dog, but had a hard time swallowing. And the more he concentrated on chewing, chewing itself became a problem.

This is all wrong. We don't need to do this. Mae doesn't need to do this.

He forced a swallow and sipped his soda, watching the level drop down in the cup. *It's not real because I can just fill it up again.*

You okay, Father?

He raised his eyes and looked at her.

You know, you don't have to eat all of that, Mae. Maybe you've ordered too much.

Father Fenton had blundered and knew it.

Mae put her pizza slab down and picked up a small napkin with her square hand and wiped her chin. Father Fenton turned away, wishing they were both back at the greeting area, like on other Fridays before the problem of food came into it.

You are going to tell me what to eat, Father? You're not even my parish priest.

Sorry Mae, I shouldn't have. Tell me about your mother. How has she been doing this past week?

I don't want to talk to you now, Father.

Mae, I've told you before, I'm a visiting priest. Jesuits aren't parish priests, remember? We're missionaries...answer only to the Pope.

I don't care who you answer to, she said, her eyes dropping down.

He wanted to touch her hand that was curled on the table next to her soda, her wide fingers blending together, but worried that would make things worse.

I'm staying at the Mission. Sometimes I say Mass there.

I've never seen you say Mass there.

She was beginning to stand, leaning her weight with her palm on the weak plastic table.

You don't go to the Mission.

Sometimes I do.

Well sometimes I say Mass at St. Patrick's or at the Nazarene. I can say Mass at any parish I want. Wherever they need help. Sometimes I say Mass in someone's home. I could say Mass at your house, Mae. Would you like that?

She rotated her body to throw her trash away, including the uneaten slice of pizza.

You could have your mother over for the Mass. It would lift her spirits. I could say it for the two of you. Where do you live again?

I don't want you saying Mass for me, Father. I don't want you visiting me anymore. I'm going back to work now. If you are so close to God, you would know this is the body He gave me.

Father Fenton didn't answer because he was wrestling with his mother for tilting his mind at an early age, making him see fat people in a way that God never would—as makers of their own bodies, too weak to help themselves. He had fallen away from seeing all bodies as God's vessels and couldn't climb out of it, which was sinful. *I am a Godmiserable man. Unable to love in all ways, like the Holy Him.*

Father Fenton wanted to say aloud—I am not Him! Because he knew he had to repudiate his pride before he could truly know Mae or anyone.

Filth, he wanted to say. I am filth. And he wanted Mae to hear it, if only she would stop moving away. But nothing can stop that. *And I, Father Fenton, have failed at the big box store, with failing for good not far off. Each mistake made worse because not flesh of the Son, but flesh of the flesh, turned waste. And a priest isn't able to forgive himself, because he cannot hear his own confession.*

If only food had never come into it. And if only he and Mae could be back at the store's entrance, not even thinking in the direction of food or the windy cheap tables or the dollar-fifty sausage….

Her back was to him as she pulled open the Costco door. Magnificent in her being, he thought, which he had never apprehended before. He had only felt pity…. Easier to forgive than be forgiven, Father Don says.

Maybe he could write Mae a letter, on Jesuit letterhead. Tell her of her magnificence. But Father Fenton didn't know Mae's last name.

Remember me, Mae, if it is worth your while. And it is Father Fentaung, like the French. After some time, anyone can remember that.

A fellow worker, with glasses and long straight hair, stared at him like she knew what he had done. What he had said.

He waved. She did not wave back. *Maybe Mae could invite her, too, to the Mass with Mae's mother.*

He stood and walked toward his car, firm in his commitment not to look back. Minutes later, he turned left from the parking lot onto Los Osos Valley Road, driving into the strong afternoon wind blowing inland from the Pacific Ocean. His hands felt numb on the steering wheel, and he was still hungry and thirsty. *I should have drunk some water. And finished my sausage dog.*

Measured rows of grapevines appeared to his right, unraveling in sportive lines into the brown California hills. He would like to choose just one of the rows and walk down it through time…. But how to know which row to pick?

Broccoli fields appeared on his left, and eventually the dirt road that led to the camp. He drove slowly, trying to avoid the rocks and ditches, believing that his Friday would be redeemed with his afternoon Mass for the Mexican field workers.

At the open-air shed, Soncia was waiting for him. The workers were out in the fields for another half hour, which was fine since Father Fenton needed time to set up. As always, he would try not to look at Soncia's hands because he was in love with them—thin and light brown…as if God made Soncia's hands to show Father Fenton what perfection looked like in a person most people would never notice. Sometimes his Mass preparation was all about finding ways to touch them, perhaps as she handed him the purificator—the rectangular piece of linen they folded lengthwise three times. Or maybe when she helped him on with his floor-length white alb or with the green stole he wore over it, the sturdy panel of cloth suspended from his neck and shoulders but never seeming to fit right until her hands adjusted it for him, and he could feel her delicate fingers vaguely touching his skin through the layers of cloth.

This time, however, it was Soncia's wrist that caught Father Fenton's attention, as she rested her arm across the white linen corporal. He had to fold the corporal into a five-inch shape to sit atop the pall, which sat atop the chalice, and there had to be some way he could accidentally brush against her thin perfect wrist. Perhaps later, when he was alone, he would kiss the corporal where her wrist had rested. Because nothing greater would ever happen to Father Fenton.

Soncia carried over some smooth rocks so the precious linens wouldn't blow away with the hot wind passing underneath the shed. Together, they unpacked the other items and laid them on the old wooden table that would serve as an altar under the shadow of the corrugated metal roof—the candlesticks and wine and water cruets, the bowl and cloth for the washing of his hands, the ciborium with the altar breads, and finally the chalice and paten.

When they finished, Soncia sat on a stool next to the wooden altar table, her remarkable hands resting on her lap and Father

Fenton, wrung out from his meditations upon her, retreated to the side of the shed to wait for the workers to arrive.

Diego entered first and took off his hat with the neck-scarf attached to the back. The others followed, all looking dusty and exhausted. Father Fenton was unsure whether Soncia was Diego's sister or his wife, because she wore no ring. And he would never know because he understood such little Spanish.

She rose to meet the workers, hugging Diego and handing out cups of water. Father Fenton wished he had a cup of water, too.

After a few minutes, he stepped behind the table.

Let us begin la misa. Queridos amigos, muy buenas tardes! Comenzamos la santa misa, en el nombre del Padre, del Hijo, y del Holy Spirit.

Father Fenton's Spanish would run out after a few lines, but the workers didn't mind. And for the first time all day, Father Fenton felt at peace, like he was doing what he was meant to do on a Friday, ministering to people no one else would reach. The litany of the Mass was flowing from him in the presence of the Spirit. He could feel it, even if they didn't fully understand his words, because they would still recognize the miracle of the consecration into flesh and blood. Like when the Mass was in Latin and he was a boy learning to serve, and no one but the priest really knew what he was doing with his back to them and it didn't matter.

Father Fenton's eyes surveyed the shed…the wearied field workers, fifteen or twenty of them sitting on chairs. But where was Soncia? Did she not stay for his Mass?

A moment later, he nearly spilled the water cruet because he wasn't paying attention. But his recitation brought him back—

Lord God almighty, creator of all life, of body and soul, we ask you to bless this water: as we use it in faith; forgive our sins and save us from all illness and the power of evil.

Lord, in your mercy give us living water, always springing up as a fountain of salvation: free us, body and soul, from every danger, and admit us to your presence in purity of heart.

Grant this through Christ our Lord…

He waited for their amen, and when he didn't hear it, he said it for them in his mind and turned to set the cruet down.

*May almighty God cleanse us of our sins, and through the Eucharist we celebrate make us worthy to sit at his table in his heavenly kingdom.... And as we prepare to celebrate the mystery of Christ's love, let us acknowledge our failures and ask the Lord for pardon and strength, for he is full of gentleness and compassion. My brothers and sisters, as we prepare ourselves to celebrate the sacred mysteries, let us call to mind our sins....*å

Father Fenton knew he had blundered. He had said too much at once. Confused, he had mixed "asking for pardon and strength" with the second liturgical option—"gentleness and compassion my brothers and sisters." And that's when he lost his place.

But he climbed back on board with—*Lord, show us your mercy and love.* Again he waited for them to say amen, and this time he said it aloud for them.

May almighty God have mercy on us, forgive us our sins, and bring us to everlasting life...

The Lord have mercy, Christ have mercy, the Lord have...

Again, they didn't repeat his recitation. But he thought he could hear the Latin from somewhere...echoing from their heavy faces against the corrugated roof of the shed—*Kyrie eleison, Christe eleison, Kyrie eleison....*

He noticed Diego holding the shoulder of an old man next to him who had apparently fallen asleep. The old man, too, must have heard the Latin chant—*Kyrie eleison, Christe eleison, Kyrie eleison....*

And Father Fenton heard his own words in Latin...as a boy, serving Mass for his father's friend, Father Coleman Daly, from whom Father Fenton got his middle name. Father Coleman Daly, in charge of the Jesuit missions all over the world, yet saying Mass in their living room because that's how special they were. With highballs to follow, and dinner...and his mother bending over to whisper, reminding him to memorize his Latin until he would never forget it.

Padre! Padre Fenton! Padrecito! Enrique no respira! Salvalo, Padre Fenton. Enrique no respira!

The old man's head was on Diego's lap. Father Fenton wanted to help but couldn't understand what Diego was saying. He considered finishing his recitation and then seeing what was the matter, but he had lost his place again.

Padre Fenton, Enrique no respira! Salvalo! Diego cried out again.

Soncia appeared from outside the shed and rushed toward Diego. She hugged the fallen man and yelled to one of the workers—

Anda, llama a una ambulancia!

She turned toward Father Fenton.

He is not breathing, Father. They want you to do something quickly. For his soul. Sí, Diego?

Sí…Padre, necesita los ritos de los muriendos, Diego said, standing and allowing Enrique's head to rest in Soncia's hands.

Hurry, Father, Soncia pleaded. Enrique is Diego's nino.

Nino?

Godfather. He is Diego's godfather. Los ritos de los Mureiendos. Last rites, Father. Please!

Padrecito, por favor, Diego said. Llama a diosito que vienne a salvar Enrique! Padre…

But I have not done the last rites, los ritos, in a long time. I am a Jesuit and we rarely…

Father Fenton was shaking as he spoke, and sweating. He tried not to look at Soncia or the dying man, but past them somewhere….

A priest never forgets, Soncia said with impatience, trying to get him to look at her.

Yes, he said. Yes….

He moved toward Enrique. *Maybe I should touch the old man's forehead.*

Por favor, Padre, favor de algo hacer. You don't have to know the Spanish, Father. Just los ritos de los Mureiendos, in English, Soncia pleaded.

He finally looked at her, hoping she would kiss him on the cheek.

I will go to my car to get the oil stock I need, he said with reluctant decisiveness. Special oil for los ritos!

Diego and another man were already lifting Enrique up. They paused next to Soncia who touched Enrique's neck for a pulse. Father Fenton thought he saw Enrique's eyes shutter open for a moment with that faraway look only the near dead have.

Él es muerto, Padre, Soncia said quietly. The ambulance can do nothing, but you still can. Favor de salvar su alma. Sí?

Maybe I should place an alter bread into his mouth, even though it hasn't been consecrated, which might not matter to them.

Instead, he touched Diego's forearm. But he and Enrique kept on moving until they left the shed.

Yes. I will run right now to my car and get the oil, he said to Soncia.

Gracias, Padre. Gracias.

Soncia touched his hand before she ran to catch up with Diego; Father Fenton's body rushed into flames.

Outside the shed, in the gauzy sunlight, Father Fenton paused to mark their procession moving up the dirt road, heading toward an RV that Father Fenton had never noticed before, parked under some eucalyptus trees. *Thank God I don't live in one of the migrant shacks,* he thought, before turning toward his car.

After starting the engine and putting up the windows, Father Fenton yelled—Idiot! You should have learned the last rites. Because this could have happened anytime. Jesus Christ! I am lost.

For he had only learned how to say Mass…later adding on confession, which was easy. Every other Friday, before his 4:00 p.m. Mass, he would listen to the Mexicans tell their sins in Spanish while sitting in a chair on the other side of the altar table that Soncia set up for him. Even though he couldn't understand what they were confessing, he always knew the prayers of penance that he gave them were exactly right.

As the last of the procession entered Enrique's RV, he drove quickly down the dirt road, not caring about the bumps and potholes and dust. He wanted to look through the mirror to see if anyone was watching him, but didn't.

He would never say Mass at the shed again; never see any of them again. Never see Soncia…all because of Enrique, the poor old man.

He wanted to cry but would not let himself…remembering his Jesuit uncle, Father Al, telling him one time—If a Jesuit cries, there really is no hope.

He lamented the Mass items left behind that had taken so long to gather and that he would never be able to replace—the paten and ciborium, stolen from the Nazarene, the altar breads he snuck away on Sunday when he served as Eucharistic Minister. What would Diego and his friends do with them, he wondered, have them with their Mexican dinner? And the candlesticks and cruets he would never find again at an antique store. And the altar cloths and chalice, the purificator and corporal….

He should have learned about all of the sacraments before going out on Fridays or at least had the stock oil for the Last Rites. Because a priest should always be prepared, like a doctor.

Back on Los Osos Valley Road, Father Fenton put down the window. He was still sweating. He considered stopping to take off his alb and stole, putting them back in the toolbox in his trunk and dusting the car with a rag so his wife wouldn't wonder how he managed to get it so dirty doing errands on his day off.

He also needed an explanation for her friend, Laura, who probably recognized him when she crossed Higuera Street in front of his car. But who would believe he was spending his Fridays driving around town dressed as a priest?

He could never be like Father Don, the parish priest at the Nazarene, where his wife managed the church money because she was such an excellent accountant. Father Don…phoning at all hours and his wife dropping everything to run to the rectory…making Father Fenton wish that, for just one day, she would rush with the same urgency and feverish eyes to be with him. But only priests were special to her.

I must get her by 6:00 p.m., he muttered aloud. I can't be late.

It was only a twenty-minute drive to her office in South County. There was still time.

He turned left onto O'Connor Road, heading in the opposite direction of his wife's office and slowed the car down since he wasn't sure. There was only notfatherfenton now…riding his bicycle to the health department four days a week in the flex-time program that saved the county money. And notfatherfenton doing errands on Fridays. Notfatherfenton who, in the course of time, would run into Jerry and Rostrum and Mae…and they would still think he was Father Fenton, but without his collar. Unless his wife was with him, then disaster would follow. So he would have to pack his lunch every day and avoid restaurants and the main streets of town.

And he would never know when they died, with old Rostrum the first to go, maybe at this very moment. So perhaps he should keep his collar on and go to see if Rostrum was all right and not worry about cleaning off the car or picking up his wife. Let Father Don get her…let Father Don take her back to his rectory while Rostrum sits with eyes closed in front of the ice cream store. Behind thick lenses, everyone walking by thinking he is napping, his head tilted to the left and the violin resting on his chest, the bow still in his crooked fingers. And the bag full of oranges, apples, pears… leaning against his leg.

Fenton's car, diminished by the expanding landscape, moved slowly around the bend where the Benedictine Monastery rose up on the right. He always wanted to go there but never had. Several times, he had driven half way up the hill before shifting into reverse and backing down.

This time I will go all the way. Walk right in and say, Take me, I will do whatever you want…give up everything, give up being Father Fenton. I will become nothing, for you. Because the Benedictines were a kind order, simultaneously dedicated to the autonomy of self and the absolute authority of the group, living in near silence under the serene blue air with the mesmerizing murmur of bees all around because he had seen their white honey hives lodged in the tall grass along the hill that sometimes appears purple in the late afternoon light.

And it would never be what he envisioned as a boy, dreaming of Jesuitical life, answering to no one but the Pope while living inside a pristine moment of purpose few others would ever know…not worrying about self love or soul murder because the Jesuits are the crème de la crème, his father used to say. The crème de la crème....

With my collar still on, and my alb and green stole, the monks will welcome my ascent. Surely, no Jesuit has given himself up to them before.

He pulled into the dirt at the bottom of the drive and looked at the sign—The Monastery of the Risen Christ—a Benedictine Community.

So, Fenton, what did you accomplish today, besides dirtying up the car and wasting gas?

He wasn't sweating anymore as he made the turn and headed up the hill, thinking about the grand cathedral in Normandy he visited when he was twenty-three after taking the train from Paris. Inside the damp cold walls, at the dusk-end of the day, he was solus ipse...paling into the penumbra of the pews as the French priest made his rounds, locking the heavy wooden front doors.

After dusting off the ancient altar stones, the priest turned and spoke the French slowly, so he would understand. In the descending cathedral darkness, the priest's face gradually faded into the altar's expanding shadow and he was expected to follow...and live inside the ancient stones, speaking French, and the Latin Vulgate that he had never forgotten.

Did you fritter your time away again this Friday, Fenton? Did you?

At the top of the monastery hill, he pulled onto the rough cobblestones and turned off the engine. A man dressed in a white shirt and dark pants, not looking monk-like, waved to him from the front garden. He didn't wave back because he still wasn't sure. But he got out of the car and the monk started walking his way, waving again. This time he waved back.

He has seen my priestly garments. And he will ask, and I will say I am Father Fenton, and I would like to....

...And the men in Belgium, who weren't priests, secretly saying Mass, because the Church was so sick there...and the Pope, furious about the hidden ecclesias...laymen breaking the bread of Jesus and training for the sacraments, so there would be no fear of los ritos, or driving away from Enriques.... But who can speak Dutch?

When the monk's feet left the garden and crossed onto the cobblestones, Father Fentaung wanted to yell—Désolé, mais je suis perdu.

But he stepped back into his car, started the engine, and quickly drove down the hill thinking—*I need to get her by 6:00 p.m., because there are no more excuses.*

Near the intersection of O'Connor Road and Foothill Boulevard, he pulled over to take off his alb and stole, but not his cassock. He grabbed a rag from the trunk and wiped the dust from the sides of the car.

A vehicle slowed into the gravel behind him. He was afraid to look back.

They think I am a priest having trouble with my car.

He motioned for them to move on because he wasn't Father Fenton anymore. But their tires ground closer into the gravel, startling a garter snake that shot out from the dead brush onto the asphalt, right past his leg. He thought he could hear other animals as well, coming out in the falling dusk. Sudden wisps and twists in the straw grass, and then…nothing. Not even the wind.

A car door opened behind him, but he ignored it and got back into his car. He wanted to return to the monastery. I will, he tried to say, but the words didn't come out.

He turned on the engine and then remembered the dust on the tires. *She will surely see that and berate me.* But he didn't want to get out of the car again.

Chapter Four
HELENA

Helena! he called to her again, using her name to demonstrate how familiar he was with her.

And she walked over to him, thinking, *He already has everything he wants—coffee, bagel, cream cheese....*

Helena, I wonder if I could get some butter, unless that's too much trouble for you, Helena.

His voice sounded slightly foreign and tired. He was in his early forties, but below his light brown bangs he had the skin of a child—soft, slightly pink, with cheeks that never seemed to have known a razor.

Helena was certain he would stare at her as soon as she turned to walk away. She could always sense his faint blue eyes from behind round wire glasses, finding their way under the edge of her black skirt, and then upward, toward the inside of her.

She brought him a small white ramekin of butter that she had smoothed perfectly across the top. Then she walked away backward so he couldn't see through her from behind. *He will have to face me if he wants to stare.*

He looked away.

From the distance of the coffee bar, Helena watched him for a few minutes, bothered by his confident wasting of time. *He never does anything, no fingering a laptop or reading the newspaper or a book...just his soft eyes lolling around. For what?*

She nearly hated him in that moment. And then derided herself for feeling that way, because her religion couldn't bear the hating of anyone.

She passed through the kitchen where Fernando was unloading pastries and Rosy was at the sink. Helena wished she could be friends with both of them but didn't know how. Fernando spoke little English and Rosy was shy. Every evening when they left work together, Helena wished she could go home with them. She wasn't even sure they lived together. But if they did, Helena wished she could sleep on their couch rather than alone in her one-room Chicago apartment.

Inside the bathroom, Helena resisted looking into the mirror as she washed her hands. Because she knew it was always a trap. She looked everywhere but at the pale reflection in the glass, even counting the number of curled black hairs on the beige tile floor. Anything other than the too-close terrain of moon flesh that couldn't be Helena. Her eyes tried to miss, as well, the small gold cross suspended between the dark blue collars of her blouse, glinting and slightly swaying just above her imperfect marbled skin.

When she returned to the café, he was gone. *Did he leave because I walked away backward?* Helena wondered.

Everything at his table appeared the same. The bagel was untouched, the cream cheese unopened, the napkin perfect, the water—not a sip taken. But the ramekin of butter had been disturbed, a stab of it missing from the center. Yet his utensils were clean. He must have used one of his thin fingers, Helena concluded. The image disturbing her....

The note was folded under a ten dollar bill left on the corner of the table—*There is something about your paleness, even where the sun touches. Your perfect white legs that one man loves like no other.*

Helena didn't see him at the coffee shop the next day, giving her hope she might never see him again.

The People Build office was in a neighborhood Helena hadn't been to before. The glass front door was reinforced with metal bars and inside, a heavy-set woman with teased orange hair sat at a steel desk.

Hang on a minute, the woman said before Helena had a chance to speak.

I just wanted to know if you had any volunteer opportunities.

Have a seat there.

The woman's computer was on, but she was looking at a paperback resting across the keyboard. Helena waited a few more minutes, then asked again.

I just need to know if—

The director will be back. You can talk with her.

When?

I'm not sure.

It was already getting dark and Helena worried about catching her bus. She considered saying, Thanks, I'll come back another time or, Here is my number, could you have the director call me? But she left without saying anything, which was so unlike Helena that she wondered if her old self was somehow floating away.

Even with two bus connections, she managed to reach the bike shop before it closed at 5:30 p.m. Helena was getting better at transiting around the alien city.

The sign above said Bike COalition, but Helena still thought of it as a bike shop. There were a lot of brochures about Bicycle Safety and Supporting Bike Paths and Bike Education Workshops and Bike Valet Services, but she just wanted a second-hand bike to use on Sundays when they closed some of the streets in downtown Chicago, and maybe even to ride to work at the coffee shop.

Henry, the shop manager, had told her the COalition didn't sell bikes. But after chatting a while, he said he had an old one he could fix up for her as long as she let him teach her how to maintain the bike herself. Helena wasn't interested in that but said okay.

When she walked in, Henry was bent over a bike seat, his long thin wisps of hair hanging toward the floor.

Your bike's not ready yet, he said without raising his head.

But tomorrow is Sunday and I wanted—

I need to know that the bike is safe for you.

Helena looked around. The only other person in the shop was a thin older man in a yellow T-shirt sitting on a low stool and tinkering with his front tire. His bike had blue storage bags slung over the rear wheel, both were heavily stained.

When Henry went into the back room, the yellow-shirted man stood and headed toward the door with his bicycle. The side of his face was tan and weathered-looking, his thin gray hair slicked behind his ears. *He is not as old as I thought.*

After passing her, he turned around to hand her a card, gazing up long enough for Helena to see that one of his eyes was lazy to the right. He nodded his head, then quickly exited the COalition.

What did he give you? Henry asked, standing close behind her.

Helena showed him the card, creased and smudged on the corner where the man's thumb had touched it. The words—Bicyclette Erotica—were in the center, and below an insignia of a tiny heart at the center of a spoked wheel. On the bottom right, a phone number.

He's from France, Henry said, turning to work on his bike again. I've told him to stop handing those things out or he couldn't come back here.

Helena wanted to tell Henry about the smell the man had as he passed—an unlikely odor of freesia.

What does this mean? Helena asked, holding up the card.

Henry moved like he was going to take the card from her, then turned toward the counter.

I think it's some club he was part of in Paris, and now he wants to start one in Chicago.... Who knows what they do. Maybe sex on a stationary cycle!

He laughed in a self-dismissive way.

Seriously, I have no idea what it's about.

Maybe we could meet sometime for lunch or coffee, Helena said.

Who? You and him? Henry asked in a joking way. Or you and me?

After a pause he continued.

Yes, maybe we could meet some evening for a beer.

Okay. Goodbye then, Helena said, wishing she had asked for the name of a bar he likes to go to.

She waved and walked out into the darkness.

Helena was hungry when she got back to her apartment but didn't feel like cooking. She thought of lying down but was afraid she would wake up more depressed. So she sat in one of the two chairs in her tiny studio and dropped her head back. With half-closed eyes, she stared at the only painting in her furnished room—a rural scene that included an old villa outside a French village. A narrow path led from the old white stucco building down to a disappearing road. The painting was simply titled *Pont-Authou*. Helena wanted to get a map of France, perhaps at the library, and see if she could find Pont-Authou.

Behind closed eyes, she could see herself walking up to the French villa, the long-combed grass spilling in from the sides of the path. She would knock at the door to see if she could rent a room there, and He would answer in words beyond hearing. And even though she couldn't see Him, she would know that He said yes.

You can stop worrying now, Helena. All the dead stones lead here....

She would look up from the portico at the warm sky spread out in layers like smoothly ironed cloth, then move inside, up the staircase to the second floor. Only by touching could she find her way. And on the other side of the wall he would be on his bed. Because, like Sister Regina said, He will lead you to someone else in His name.

...And it will feel like I've always known Him. He will whip the bright air for me until I can breathe light, that arcs for a moment allowing me to pass through, before the sky and clouds turn to stone....

There was no name or date on the painting, but for some reason Helena believed it had been painted recently, maybe by the landlord himself, a Frenchman whose name she couldn't remember. She could call and ask him about the painting, but he had never answered her when she complained about the loud vibrations coming from inside the radiator, like some frenzied demon was trying to get out.

The card was still in her hand. As Helena set it on the wooden table by the door, she sensed that the yellow-shirted man was already watching her from across the room. Because it had nothing to do with bicycles...*and she could watch her body with him, a body she didn't recognize as her own...and he wasn't the man in the yellow shirt, but the stranger from the other side of the wall, revealed by Him, with clean hands because that's all she would ask for...his voice without words telling her how to lay herself down, with eyes still closed, seeing by touching....*

Helena put three eggs on to boil, then turned on the shower, avoiding her body as she passed the mirror. When she got out, she returned to the stove without grabbing her towel to dry off. The eggs had not cooked long enough, but that didn't matter. She cooled them under running water, peeled the white shells, and dashed the eggs with salt and pepper. The whole time her body was dripping on the counter and floor. The insides were soft and runny, but Helena only thought, *too much salt*, and poured herself a glass of milk.

She left the shells by the sink and lay on her bed. Within seconds, her wet body felt cold and the dampness from her hair filled the pillow around her. *Moving will be painful, like wet fire on prickly skin.*

Helena let herself sink deeper with closed eyes, so she couldn't see any of the flesh, waiting for the dim shapes to begin to move... and take over.

When she awoke, the room was dark and she was shivering. Helena dressed in layers, forgoing her bra for a shirt and two sweaters over her chilled skin. After putting on her long coat, she headed out into the March night.

She had passed O'Grady's dozens of times over the last month, and it looked like the kind of place that would make her nervous. So after entering, she quickly aimed for an open seat at the bar, next to the waitress station. When the bartender—a short muscular man with facial hair around his thin lips—asked what she wanted, Helena said, Vodka tonic, because that's what the man next to her had just ordered.

Helena sipped it quickly, trying to convince herself she had ordered wisely. But every time she lifted the glass, she could see herself in the mirror above the bottles, which was a problem. Helena didn't want to give up her stool, so she trained herself to look to the right as she drank, keeping her eyes moving so she wouldn't stare at anyone in particular, while nervously pressing the liquid down inside her...telling herself not to leave O'Grady's, not to leave

Chicago, and not to see her family in Duluth like she had promised her superiors she was going to do.

A man with a crew cut, not much more than twenty, ordered a Jameson on the rocks and asked if he could buy Helena a drink. She avoided looking at him and shook her head, letting her hair fall across her face like a dark veil. She didn't stop shaking until he finally moved away. Then she ordered a Jameson on the rocks.

Good for you, the bartender said with a slight smile. You chose the Catholic one rather than the protestant one.

Helena didn't know what he meant, but the Catholic one felt like fire in the back of her throat. Helena liked that and wished the fire was real.

She ordered another Jameson and this time the bartender gave her a glass of water with it that Helena was afraid to drink because she needed to use the bathroom but didn't want to give up her stool. So she took only small sips, forgetting about the mirror for a second and accidentally seeing the woman who looked like a bird with perky lips flush on the edge of the glass.

Helena corrected her posture, slipped off her coat, and whispered to herself—*I am at O'Grady's, near where I have my own apartment…near where I work. And as long as He is still watching me, everything will be okay.*

She needed someone to explain it to…maybe a stranger. But she kept moving her head back and forth every time someone approached.

Could you save my seat while I use the bathroom? Helena asked the waitress.

Honey, just put a napkin over your drink.

After using the toilet, Helena washed her hands while ducking away from the mirror. Then dried her hands on her pants because there weren't any towels. She tried to hurry back through the crowd but there was already a man with a cap leaning against her stool.

Excuse me, she said, and took her seat from the other side.

But he continued to lean, as if Helena and the stool were a wall post.

I know you, he said, looking at the woman in the mirror.

Outside the mirror, Helena started shaking her head.

I'll remember…. Give me a minute.

After enough shaking, he moved away, and Helena ordered another Jameson. The bartender said she would have to drink it quickly because they were closing soon. And Helena did, because she didn't want to disappoint him, clinging to her stool as long as she could and eventually putting her head down to rest for just a minute, until he touched her shoulder and they walked out of O'Grady's together. It is too late to be on the streets alone, he said.

He accompanied her up the stairs, letting Helena lean on him. She smelled the tobacco on his jacket, reminding her of when her father used to carry her up to bed.

After switching on the light, she realized he was not as young as she thought, and that he looked across her face rather than into her.

All right, he said. Make sure you drink some water before you go to sleep.

Helena tried to touch his lips with hers, to see if they tasted like tobacco, but fell into his shoulder. His right arm caught her, his left hand pressed into her back.

You are beautiful, and you don't wear makeup, he said softly, like he was worried someone might hear.

Below, Helena felt him pushing against her. She flinched away, lost her balance and fell sideways onto the bed, her hair across her face so she couldn't see him, but still waiting for him to kiss her goodnight through her hair, like her father used to do.

Instead, she heard his footsteps descending the wooden stairs. Helena counted them, hearing them pause for a long moment, and then continue.

I have to get up and close the door…. But she didn't move. She didn't want to undress either, because her clothes would protect her from the dampness in the sheets. Helena tried to remember why the sheets were damp, but couldn't.

Sunday afternoon seemed to stretch out forever. And it felt like everyone else's Sunday afternoon, not Helena's. The COalition was closed, and she was disappointed she couldn't ride her bike. So she walked slowly to Seward Park.

She sat across from the fountain and rested her head on the back of the bench. To her left, some kids were taking boxing lessons on the grass; behind her, some young men were playing basketball, their shoes grinding on the asphalt, the dribbling ball rattling Helena's nerves.

She still felt sick from the night before and wanted to sleep. But two squirrels near Helena's feet looked like they were plotting to do something the second she closed her eyes.

In the distance, she could see the empty expanse where Cabrini Green used to be, the final tower only recently imploded. *All the people removed. But to where? Because I could have helped some of them if they would have let me.*

Sister, I am going to Cabrini Green. Whatever happens…. And the depressing corridors moved past Helena's eyes like horizontal escalators with people staring, wondering what her dead white face was doing there….

Sister, I am going to Cabrini Green, where the people come out of doorways that have no numbers, but I will know the right one… through the thousands of dimly lit corridors with clouds of smoke hovering above…into the small apartment that has no furniture except a stripped bed and a dresser without drawers…and I won't say I am there to help, because he will already know…lay down, Sister, and after that you can help me…I'm trying to figure if the others who came before did the same thing, because nobody really knows someone else's past….

You can't, Sister. No one lives in Cabrini Green anymore….

Still she waits, leaning against the empty dresser.

I want to say yes, because then I can help. But the surface of the bed is difficult to see. This is how it must feel without clothes…when there is no dampness, moving without sound, and he, ready to touch.

The pounding dribble of the basketball convinced Helena that she had to move. The squirrels, four or five of them now, still watching.

You would think everything would be beautiful here, wouldn't you, Sister? With a name like Cabrini Green…an infinite lawn where the martyrs and saints get to play, and the squirrels tunneling underneath to fortify everything, and that's why the towers can't fall and why the ground feels so solid in Chicago....

She walked past the amateur boxers learning how to punch each other's beautiful faces, around the fountain where a flock of sparrows kept flying through the high-spouting water. *Impossible, because birds never want to get their wings wet.*

She dragged a bench up against the fountain so all she could hear was the sound of water. And, after a while, with closed eyes, she couldn't hear anything.... Thinking, this would be a good time to be lifted up.

When she awoke, he was sitting next to her.

Helena wondered how long he had been watching her face, and how near he had been to her closed eyes.

What is your name? Helena asked, her head still back on the bench, her body feeling like it was too heavy to move.

What is your last name? he asked.

Helena dropped her eyes down to see his hand—a small white thing scrubbed so clean it appeared raw in places—moving closer, like a sea creature, an anemone.

Why did you do that to the butter? she asked. It upset me.

Helena kept her arms crossed and watched as his hand slowly retreated.

I needed to get your attention.

Helena rolled her head away and noticed how much the light had changed while she had slept. It was nearly twilight.

What is your last name? he asked again, his voice almost a whisper.

Trafalger, she said, because it seemed he had already won and there was nothing her body could do.

Helena Trafalger, he chanted.

Helen, she said, still looking away.

But you are Helena, no?

Why are you always staring at me, and why do you—

They made me this way, he interrupted, his light blue eyes, behind round lenses, looking away as if he was embarrassed.

Who?

But I could be kind with you, Helena, he said, his eyes returning. That's why I need to be with you. You will make me kind.

The wind shifted and some of the fountain spray was hitting Helena's hair and his glasses, but he didn't seem to notice.

Did you follow me?

I always walk in Seward Park on Sunday, but it's the first time I've seen you here. It was meant to be, Helena Trafalger, saying her name like it was an incantation.

Stop that, she said.

Helena sat up, her eyes fully opened. She moved close to his child-like face.

I am leaving now, she said, and stood in a shuffling manner, her body not quite responding to her will.

She never looked back as she walked, but she knew he was there, staring through her from behind. For the first time, Sister Helen was completely gone, which was what Helena had wanted for weeks. But now, wistfully, she wanted part of her back. *Where are you, Sister?* Like the old man with dementia at the Emerald Isle Support Home, where Helena first worked when she arrived in Chicago, screaming, Where is Sister Helen? Where is Sister Helen? after she told him her name was now Helena and Sister Helen wasn't coming back. She tried to calm him by showing him her cross.

He seemed familiar with her apartment, like he had visited when she wasn't home. After dropping his coat on the back of the chair next to her bed, he barely looked around. Helena stared at the painting of Pont-Authou, going there with her eyes while her hands patiently removed her clothes. She could sense him across the small room, watching her, but didn't care anymore.... *And after you lay down, Sister, I will let you help me....*

Helena fell back onto the cold sheets with eyes open. She was on her way to Pont-Authou and didn't pay attention to the man undressing and removing his glasses. And when he began slowly kissing his way up her legs, she was already on her way up the path to the villa, the soft wind billowing like dry white sheets, lifting Helena toward Him with "time swift as the weaver's shuttle," as Elohim likes to say…which is why she wanted him to move quickly inside her, but he couldn't leave her *perfect white legs, that one man loves like no other…*and she couldn't move herself, because Sister Helen's body wasn't hers anymore.

All her life, she had thought it would be Him. She had worn His silver ring…through all the years teaching her fourth grade classes and walking back to the convent with nothing there for her but waiting for Him, expecting Him to say one evening, *Now is the time, Sister….*

And then to hear Sister Regina, in her last breath, say, He will never come to you at the Convent, Sister, even though you wear his ring. You will have to leave, like I never did.

She called to Him as he touched to move her apart, his naked eyes closed after so much staring…cupping his small raw hand lightly over her mouth so she wouldn't call to Him again. And she, unable to see Pont-Authou anymore with him rising up in between, arching above Helena who was bare necked because she had removed her cross along with her clothes—and who can see around shoulders with too many bones and not enough flesh?—moving like the weaver's shuttle, and him still not letting her say His name, so she whispered in Hebrew because it was more pure—*Yeshua, Yeshua*—never doubting that it was Him who did the calling, urging her to find a place on her own, away from Detroit and not in Duluth…the sin making her lie to her family and her superiors… the voice of sin, and not Him, coming in dreams whenever she slept without clothes…directing her to a place where nobody would know her, and then seeing Him just once at the coffee shop, but He was already walking away because she realized it too late, and not again until weeks later, seeing Him through the painting of Pont-Authou, because He had become French for her so that Helena could be with Him there, through the body of the man on the other side of the wall.

His eyes squinted tight as if he was in pain during the final moments, the blood sweat dripping from his forehead upon her breasts, and the flesh of her self feeling different as he lowered his spent face back down upon her thighs, unaware that Helena

Trafalger was vanishing, like a spiral shutter closing, with Sister Helen left behind, too. And she, on the other side of the painting, moving with Him now...His tan beatific hand inside hers, the villa fading into clouds as they walked without clothes across the silvery water under a white still sky...she, gazing at her body as if seeing it for the first time, but not looking at Him, because in that second, she feared, He might disappear.

She was determined to remain still for as long as it took him to leave, but she moved her legs from under him instead, feeling herself in that moment becoming the flesh that all men desire, before she ever became Sister...seeing herself as they do—body parts leading to the final desire inside.

At age thirty-nine, without a name, beautiful without makeup, no longer even from Duluth...appearing sui generis in north Chicago. Becoming and becoming and becoming...like the ancient philosopher Heraclitus said, until, floating above the silver-white lake, she is the one who leaves, her body obeying her completely, sliding across the damp cold sheets...dressing in only the clothes she would need, and taking the painting. While his curled translucent body, half-covered by the sheet, begins to disappear the moment she turns away.

From the bedside table, she removes his glasses and leaves her cross in its place, certain he will never understand. And then she is away...moving toward Him.

Chapter Five
MCCUADE

I

I was supposed to fly to Athens, then travel by car to Sicyon on the Gulf of Corinth, and by boat through the straights of Salamis and across the Aegean, not stopping at Paros to see why Archilochus loved that island so much…to Ephesus, on the central coast of Turkey.

But McCuade got in the way.

Perhaps I don't have to go to Sicyon and Ephesus in order to write about Praxilla and Heraclitus. Perhaps I can reimagine them, conflating geography and time…Praxilla, poet and great adorant of Adonis, and lover of simple corporeal things, like cucumbers…. Heraclitus, philosopher and visionary of a universe in flux, with fire as his first principle. Yet they rejected his Logos and threw stones at him during the sixty-ninth Olympiad.

But McCuade is in the real and now. McCuade, no doubt himself a poet and a philosopher. He stands firm at Dungloe.

Through the Garage Wall Man, I can almost see him…. The sheer flesh of him overshadowing the Irish cosmos. McCuade quidditas. McCuade, the universal man.

II

Balls of hail swept across the road in front of me but never touched the little Ford diesel sedan. *Because of McCuade.*

Dark clouds rode alongside, like Irish steeds above the green fields. No other cars in sight.

According to the map, I was closing in on Dungloe. But after passing the village of Narrin and reaching the Gweebarra Bridge, a road sign said, *An Clochán Liath.*

An Clochán Liath? That bastard McCuade!

I tried refolding the map but gave up and threw it on the dashboard.

Where the hell is Dungloe? I said out loud. And why did I believe in the Garage Wall Man? *McCuade may not exist.* Perhaps the Garage Wall Man made him up because I didn't invite him into my house. And imbecile guilt made me believe him. And now, Dungloe, ceasing to exist....

After the Gweebarra Bridge, I turned to follow the water and passed another sign—*An Clochán Liath.* I wanted to curse McCuade again, but an estuary opened on my left into a peaceful tidal flat spreading toward the western horizon. I stopped the car and felt an impulse to bless myself. Hadn't performed that gesture in decades.

On a small pad of paper, I jotted down: Outside of An Clochán Liath, almost blessed myself. Don't know why. May 10, 2013.

As I pulled back onto the road, a car flew by, nearly clipping my mirror. And in that second, my quest for McCuade seemed to fritter out the window and across the dreamy tidal flats. *I am breathing McCuade out of me. Or, perhaps, McCuade is breathing himself free.*

Irish houses appeared on my right. The smell of their earthy peat fires becoming pervasive. The fuscous bogs themselves layered out under the angled sunlight.

Around a bend, I joined a line of cars that was hardly moving, as if everyone had drifted into slow-down time. The cars had their headlights on, so I put on mine. It's a funeral procession, I decided.

A final sign appeared, my car almost standing still next to it—*An Clochán Liath / Welcome to Dungloe.*

The tourism office in Donegal told me the Dungloe B&Bs weren't open, since no one was going to the old fishing village anymore. When I called one of the numbers, just to see, an old woman answered and said her B&B was closed because she was sick. Maybe I was in her funeral procession.

After passing a small grocery store, the cars increased their speed. My God, that's it? That was Dungloe?

A narrow, unmarked road that wasn't on the map appeared to my left, and I decided to turn around and take it. A few moments later, I was down in a valley along the north Atlantic Sea, and the real Dungloe suddenly rose up before me. *This is why the B&Bs are closed. No one knows to make that turn, so no one finds Dungloe.*

The long Main Street, with a cluster of businesses and pubs and houses on both sides, dipped almost below sea level, and then ran up a hill on the other side. Dungloe looked better than I had imagined. Like Homer's utopian land of the Phaeacians it was a true fishing village by the sea, with a wide harbor and a long jetty stretching into the illimitable blue-green.

On the other side of town, I stopped at an old gray-stucco building that had no name, but just said B&B. After ringing the bell and waiting for a while, a man answered, his face red and swollen as if someone had beaten him with a wire brush.

Yes, we are open, he said with a hoarse voice.

He led me down the hall toward some stairs. From behind, I could see that his neck had some kind of bulbous growth on it.

Is anyone else staying here now?

Soon. We will be full soon.

The second-floor carpet smelled moldy and the room itself was small and damp smelling. But it had a brilliant view of the sea.

Do you want this, then? he asked, his head craning to look up at me.

I'll come back and let you know. I'm not sure yet if I'm staying the night.

Closer to town and across from the sea jetty, was Inisean, a yellow one-story B&B with lots of flowers in the driveway. A young woman with brown straight hair answered. She was moonfaced and wore cowboy boots.

Sorry, sir. Me mum died, and we're not open for business.

Her eyes looked through the open door like she wanted to get outside.

I just need to stay one night. I won't be a bother.

She stared at me for a moment, her eyes shaped like almonds.

I'm sorry about your mom's death, I continued. I believe I paid my respects at her funeral procession today.

Mary Quinn died weeks ago, she said, her voice rising musically.

Oh.

We're not sure we're going on with the business.

I wondered about the "we." Did it include her siblings? Husband? Children? She wore no ring and looked to be about thirty.

Well, if you change your mind, I can give you my phone number and—

You can have the room in the back, she said.

The room had a large bed with lots of colorful little pillows and a window looking toward the harbor. The perfume smell made me think it had been her mother's room. She handed me a key and told me the room would be forty Euros and included an Irish breakfast.

I rested on the bed, taking the spread off first, like my mother used to tell us to do. Mary Quinn's perfume seemed to be coming from inside the mattress.

Outside the window was a flowerbox with pansies and a bird making a commotion in the trellis. It sounded like a meadowlark. I considered getting up and opening the window to shoo it away. But it stopped after a while.

...And she came in, leaned over the bed, and asked if I needed anything. Her hair hung loose on both sides of her moon face. As she got closer—her hair smelling of berry blossoms.

Do you need help finding McCuade? she whispered, touching my shoulder. And then his voice—Go ahead, you can take her. Leave her boots on....

I awoke because the meadowlark was clamoring again. After brushing my teeth and unpacking a few things, I grabbed my jacket. I needed to walk through Dungloe and ask about McCuade before it got too late.

She was in the entranceway talking on the phone. I couldn't tell if she was still wearing her boots because she had changed into a long flowing skirt.

Are you all set, sir? she asked, dropping the phone from her ear.

Thanks. I'm going into town. Looking for a man named McCuade. Have you heard of him?

There's no McCuades around here.... Sounds like a Scottish name.

What is your name?

Why, it's Mary Quinn, she said.

Ah, yes. Well, see you later, then, Mary Quinn.

As she returned to the phone, I heard her say—Strawberries. He brought me strawberries.

The late afternoon light had already set in as I walked downhill toward the main street of Dungloe, about a mile away. *I should have left sooner, because the shops will be closing and then I will only have the pubs and restaurants to ask about McCuade.*

Inside the hardware store, a skinny dark-haired boy behind the counter was playing a video game on his phone. He said he didn't know McCuade, but told me to go to Clary's Pub, because Clary knows everyone in Dungloe.

So I went to Clary's where three men sat at the bar and an old woman rested at a corner table drinking Guinness. While I waited for the bartender to be free, I gazed out the back picture window. Beyond the rear deck was a long view toward Dungloe harbor with some soccer fields in between. *I'll have to walk down there before it gets dark.*

So, you're asking about McCuade? Clary asked, standing right next to me.

He had short cropped brown hair and a thick neck. His white arms were hairless.

How did you know?

Johnny called me from the store. The lad's always trying to be helpful. Not many folks come here asking about people they don't know.

You know McCuade, then?

I knew a McCuade…wasn't from around here. Worked down at the boathouse, by the slipway.

He pointed out the picture window.

That was years ago. The boathouse is closed now, business being what it is in Dungloe.

He stared beyond me, through the window and then back at the bar like he was worried about a customer. But nobody seemed to want anything.

Maybe I'll go down to the boathouse, then.

Aye, if you like. But there'll be nobody there to help you.

And I'll come by later tonight for a pint, in case you think of anything else about McCuade.

I'll be here. But I'll have nothing else to say. McCuade is long gone.

You don't remember a first name for him, do you?

Clary had already walked away; his time with me was over.

I headed out the back door, down some stairs, through an alley, and onto the soccer fields that were soggy. I could feel the moisture seeping through to my socks. I tried running but my feet sunk deeper. So I tip-toed, hoping no one from Dungloe was watching the skinny American dancing his way toward the harbor. I looked back at the picture window of Clary's Pub, but the low sun reflecting against the glass made it impossible to tell if anyone was watching.

There was a fence at the end of the fields that I couldn't see how to get around, so I climbed over it. The shoreline had the stench of low tide and, instead of a beach, there was only black mud and some scattered large rocks. *An Irish wasteland.*

Since my shoes were already wet, I stepped through the muck and climbed one of the larger rocks. In the distance, I could see the jetty but couldn't see the boat house. *I need to get there.* But my sense of purpose seemed to drift away…*Jesus, what am I doing here?*

I considered jumping into the shallow tidewater on the other side of the rock....

McCuade not Irish, but Scottish? But making his home in Dungloe.... At the boathouse and then gone.

Was I more afraid of finding McCuade, or finding out he wasn't real?

...Strawberries, she said, he brought me strawberries....

And what American idiot would be in Dungloe rather than Greece doing the research he was paid to do? Because no one questions the value of the Greeks. But the Scottish-Irish bastard McCuade, he's a different story. A man beyond time, leading to....

I stepped down from the rock, lost my balance, then caught myself, my left foot landing in the tidal mud. *That's it. I'm going back to Inisean to change my shoes and socks. I can ask Mary Quinn for some detergent to wash them out.*

The jetty was on my way, though, and the sun would be sinking soon.

I found a path that led around to the north side of the harbor. Up against the hillside was the boathouse, a solid-looking structure made of stone. A little plaque on the side said it was originally built as a mill in 1836. The windows were boarded up and the red wooden door was locked, but I knocked anyway. Waited, knocked again...and then turned toward the jetty, trying to ignore the cold dampness in my shoes.

The sun broke through the low streaking gray clouds and the wind suddenly picked up. Within minutes it seemed gale force, coming right into the harbor from the west. I passed another plaque—*Dungloe Slipway / Officially Completed 21st October 2006.*

At the end of the slipway, the wind was so intense I marveled at a tiny sailboat tacking across the white caps, racing its way into Dungloe harbor without flipping over. The white sun was shimmering upon the boat and no longer on the slipway where my legs were like sticks I was trying to post into place. The tide was rushing in, too, in union with the wind, and the chaotic waves lapped upon the concrete near my feet.

There seemed to be a chord of music lacing through the wind if I positioned my head at just the right angle. I wondered if anyone had heard it before…a harmonious chord perhaps from the powers beyond. *Maybe this is what Pythagoras meant when he claimed he could hear the music of the spheres…now playing from a blazing sun, through a forty mile an hour Irish wind, across the slipway.*

Could this be what I came for, I wondered, *and not McCuade? Unless he led me to this point. McCuade…as emissary of the Pythagorean, playing an Irish sea harp, open to the ethereal sky and powered by the spheres…at 8:23 p.m., canonized by a slowly dying western sun.*

White light suddenly streaked upon the slipway and the water lapped higher onto my legs. The sailboat made another tack and accelerated through the white caps. The sailor, more like a god than a man, hung over the side to keep his boat magically afloat. And the vibrating chord, oscillating yet constant, continued…drawing me into a trance with the wind and sea and sun, until a violent slamming of a door ended my moment—

A man wearing a hooded red plaid jacket advanced upon the slipway, his thick legs shuffling at a steady pace. *If this is McCuade, then that bastard Clary lied. And I certainly wouldn't go back to buy a pint from him.*

The man had a mustache and a narrow, contorted face, so he didn't look like McCuade. And his eyes aimed downward like he was going about some bothersome business.

I found myself backing away and didn't know why, even though there was little room on the slipway behind me. Perhaps the gale wind, now at my back, would lift me up so the plaid-jacket man couldn't touch me.

Were you the one knocking at the boathouse door? he asked, still advancing, his narrow eyes finally focused on me.

I was looking for someone…a man named McCuade.

Aye, Clary told me. He isn't here anymore.

He continued moving forward, but in slow-motion.

Did you ever think the man you're looking for might not want to be found?

I was at the edge, the water lapping on the backs of my legs. If he threw me off the spillway, would the man in the sailboat see?

Do you know where he's gone? It's important. A dear friend is trying to find him.

You?

He finally stopped just inches away and pulled his hood tight against his ears. His square fingers were crusted with a brown stain.

He went up to Inishowen a few years ago, he said with muted hoarseness. He's from there, I think. Heard he was working at a golf course. Ballyliffin.... He was smart to leave, like lots of others. Fishin's done here in Dungloe. So, will you go back on your fookin' holiday?

He didn't wait for my answer but retreated much more quickly because the wind was at his back. I'm not on fookin' holiday, I wanted to yell. But I turned toward the water to hear the eternal music again.

I couldn't find the sound at first. Then, after moving a few steps, it was there. But it really wasn't from the spheres. It was from the three metal bars on the guardrail. They were playing the first, fourth, and fifth notes—the mystical Pythagorean chord—reverberating from the Dungloe slipway like three strings on a wind harp. And if one stood in the right place within the sunset rush of Irish wind, one could hear their call.

Moments later, the sun began to sink behind some gray clouds. The wind faded, and the music, too.

It was over.

I headed back to Inisean to wash out my socks and shoes. *Tomorrow I will go to Inishowen and I will find McCuade.*

At the Bay View Bar, I ordered a pasta shrimp dish and a pint of Guinness. And I wished I could celebrate with someone about finding evidence that McCuade was at Ballyliffin.

A band called The Logues was setting up to play, so the waitress turned the soccer match off to the complaints of a man sitting in front of me with his wife and another couple. The man abused the waitress until she walked away red-faced, and then the owner came over to quiet him, and he yelled at the owner, too. When his wife tried to step in, he pushed her away and called her a name I didn't hear because The Logues were tuning up.

After that, I couldn't focus on anything except this heavy, balding, boorish man. He seemed dissatisfied with everyone. When his friends talked, he didn't listen. Instead he looked around the room for something that might exist just for him.

His lamb chops arrived and he ate them with his hands and kept licking his fingers, then wiped them on the table cloth. *He eats like a pig*. And wished Circe herself would appear to transform him…send him off grunting to the sty.

Above his short-sleeved white shirt, his large head twisted around to look at me. He was daring me to think he was McCuade, and that the plaid-jacket man had lied about Ballyliffin.

The longer I watched him, the more grotesque he became; his broad shoulders and heavy upper body out of proportion with his thin white forearms and long fingers. When he stared at people, he was thinking of licking them.

I wanted to listen to The Logues, but the pig man had ruined everything. On the way out, I stopped by my waitress.

That man sitting in front of my table, he doesn't happen to be named McCuade, does he?

That man? she flinched. He's the son of Satan.

Could I buy him a drink, then, and would you deliver a note with it?

That would be no problem, sir.

I gave her ten Euro and wrote on a piece of paper—*I'm glad you are not McCuade, because you eat and act like a pig.*

It was cold and damp when I left the Bay View, so I put my collar up for the mile-long trek up to Inisean. I thought about turning back and watching through the window as the pig man opened my note. And then my stomach dropped away as I realized I never should have put McCuade's name on it. Everyone in town knows I've been looking for McCuade, and it wouldn't take long for him to figure out I was staying at Inisean, with the other B&Bs

closed. Since he was a local, the pig man would be able to track me down, all the way to my bedroom. Unless Mary Quinn lied and said I wasn't staying there. But why would she do that? And he could still look through my window.

I thought about knocking on Mary Quinn's bedroom door and telling her everything. Then she would ask me to sleep on the floor by her bed…*every now and then leaning over to make sure I'm still there, her brown hair hanging loose…because the man with slender fingers and bulbous head wants to drag me down to the slipway and hang me over the three-note railing, and Mary Quinn won't have the strength to deny me, because she won't be wearing her boots. But she will whisper in Irish as they drag me away, with The Logues's music echoing in the distance. At dawn, Mary Quinn comes to the end of the slipway and sits next to me with hands folded like she is posing as the Virgin, moonfaced and beautiful in the vague yellow light reflected from the water and the twinkling houses around Dungloe. There is no wind, so I can't hear the Pythagorean chord from the Eternals….*

I couldn't fall asleep because I kept listening for his car tires crunching on the gravel. But I must have dozed at some point because at 2:00 a.m. I awoke to his voice in the hallway. I stood with my Swiss Army knife in hand even though I couldn't imagine using it. His voice and Mary Quinn's, too, fluttered to the end of the hallway because that's where Mary Quinn sleeps.

And she would be naked in her bed whispering to the strawberry man, his hands on her back pressing their chests close together until they breathe as one….

After keeping watch for another hour, I decided to leave and drive through the night to Inishowen. I packed my bag and left fifty Euros on the dresser. When I opened my door, though, Mary Quinn was walking down the hallway without any clothes on, the backside of her looking just like I imagined, except that she was wearing socks because Irish girls wear socks eleven months of the year since it is always cold in Irish houses. So you only get to see their feet in July.

She turned toward the kitchen and I shut my door and lay back on my bed. *I'll wait until morning,* I decided, *because I won't be able to read the Irish street signs in the dark anyway.*

After serving my breakfast, Mary Quinn left me alone. *He's still in the bedroom, washing his fingers in the sink, waiting for me to leave.*

I returned to the hardware store, and the same boy was working there.

Can I buy more minutes for my phone?

No problem, he said. And did you find what you needed about your friend?

Yes, I'm heading north now.

His sister was arranging some small flashlights on the shelf. She looked to be about twelve and had long dark hair. *Black Irish, just like him.*

I would like one of those.

She handed me a small blue flashlight.

Thank you.

As I turned away, she said, Mister…I hope you find McCuade.

Her words killed me. Because she believed in McCuade more than I did. And I didn't want to disappoint her.

I left Dungloe, driving along the eastern side of the The Rosses, an ancient and vast expanse of rock-strewn land with over a hundred tiny lakes, then along the northern side of the Derryveagh Mountains, through the large town of Letterkenny, and north into the Inishowen Peninsula. At the top of Inishowen was the northern most point of all of Ireland—Malin Head.

Reaching Ballyliffin Golf Course around three, I thought about playing nine holes since the course was so famous. But the blustering winds and rain coming in from the northwest made me decide against it. Lots of Irish folks were out on the sand-strewn links, though, wearing full weather gear as if they were working on the bow of a ship in a storm.

In the Pro Shop, I asked about McCuade. But no one had heard of him, and I wondered if the plaid-jacket man on the spillway had lied, coerced by that bastard Clary.

After using their bathroom, I considered heading all the way back to Dungloe to deal with Clary, when I saw an old man bringing a set of golf clubs in from the rain. He had shocking white hair down to his shoulders and his back was stooped.

Sir, I said, touching him lightly on the arm. Have you ever heard of a man named McCuade working here?

I knew a greens keeper by that name, he said, not raising his head to look at me. I think he was from Scotland. Was an expert at truing the greens. A helluva golfer, too, especially at hitting low into the wind. He had a way of—

Do you know what happened to him?

Can't say for sure.... Heard he went up to Malin Head and was working on the fishing boats. But that was a while back.

What was he like? Do you remember? It's important to me.

He stared up at me, his eyes watery blue.

He was a handsome fella, never said much, and always one step ahead of everyone. And he had a temper, if things didn't go his way. I think that's why they let him go. But you'd have to ask about that inside.

I asked in there. No one knew him.

That's strange.... Well, I'll be off now. Unless you're playing a round and need a caddy.

In this rain?

Irishmen play their best golf in the rain.

I shook his thin, strong hand, turned toward the parking lot.

If you catch up with him, he continued, tell him old Riley sends his best. And remind him, he still owes me forty Euros, that laddy does.

I wanted to make it to Malin Head before the afternoon was over. I felt strangely drawn there.

It was only a thirty-minute drive through the most beautiful and mystical stretch of land and sea I had ever seen. I could feel the peninsula narrowing, thrilled by the fact there would be nowhere else for McCuade to go unless he walked across the Irish Sea.

I passed a rustic looking hotel, The Seaview Tavern, right across from the ocean, and took a room there. A woman named Caitlin answered all of my questions with—That is no problem, sir. Until I asked about McCuade, then she twisted her eyebrows and said she'd never heard of him, which didn't bother me because I could feel I was in the right place.

From my second-floor window, I had a spectacular view of the primal northern sea, and a shimmering lighthouse about five miles away on Inishtrahull Island, Ireland's most northerly island. An uninhabited pile of rocks, Caitlin said. *The last refuge....*

Caitlin said I could pay a fisherman to drop me off at Inishtrahull for the day, if the currents were right and the weather fine. But there's no food or water on the island, she cautioned. The last residents left there in 1929. And if the fisherman couldn't make it back by sunset, you'd have to spend the night there on your own.

She took my reservation for dinner at the Seaview Tavern restaurant, and then I left to see Malin Point before it got dark. The sky was overcast and spritzing with rain. I made a wrong turn, though, and found myself heading down a steep dead-end lane to the sea. The narrow road was so severe I worried about my car making it back up. So I parked and walked the rest of the way. There were two large rock outcroppings at the bottom, like twin Stonehenge pillars, and the stone ruin of a fourteenth century chapel.

Underneath some thick beach grass next to the chapel was a natural spring called the Malin Well. A sign said the water was thought to cure all diseases. I feared drinking it because of bacteria, so I rinsed my face with it and let the sun, which had just broken through the thin clouds, dry my skin.

Behind the chapel ruin was a natural cave called the Wee House of Malin. It was about ten feet deep and looked more like an alcove. A sign said a hermit once lived there and that the cave had a miraculous power—no matter how many people entered, there would always be room for more. *I will have to come back with a large group of Irish folks to see if the legend is true.*

I climbed into the cave, sat on a rock ledge, and gazed out past the chapel ruins, through the invisible gate between the two rock monoliths, to the illimitable Irish Sea. The Island of Inishtrahull and the white-washed lighthouse looked closer now, because I was near the tip of Malin Head.

I could just sleep here, rest my head on the dark soil inside the Wee House, even though my hair is still wet from the sacred stream.

I felt a debilitating exhilaration I had not known before... an expanding sense of wanting nothing more. *Maybe that's why an infinite amount of people can fit inside, because the Wee House necessitates the end of all desire... inside the present moment, where all human yearning ends, beyond the slant of time itself. And that's what the hermit must have discovered, for the millionth time—there is no goal more desirous than the present moment, yet no goal more elusive, trapped as we are by our hopes of something else beyond, resulting in our endless sense of loss, which the Irish, in particular, seemed to understand.*

I closed my eyes for as long as it took to feel the corporeal thread of time unraveling, and when I opened them, I could see his wavering body, like the shimmering lighthouse itself, moving across the water toward me, ahead of even Him, who was sure to follow.

But he was enough.

As he walked, the lighthouse slowly moved with him, as if they were bolted together under the Irish Sea, with the yellow-orange sun flashing off the waves in blinding streaks. And he—calm, rubbing his chin, turning his head to the left and right, as if he was thinking.

I surveyed the cave walls to make sure I wasn't moving as well, and when I gazed back to the sea, he was gone. *He has already retreated back to Inishtrahull. And what a fool I was to think he would sit across the cave from me and, together, we could become the miraculous Irish multitude.*

My vision, empty of all desire, had been miscast. *Because I haven't traveled far enough. And that's why McCuade disappeared from the closest I've ever been. Unless he never was, and I vainglorious....*

I picked up four tiny stones and pressed them into the soft clay wall in a diamond shape. *If I ever come back, they will prove that I was here.* In the same moment I heard footsteps out on the shore rocks. I stepped out of the Wee House, walked past the old chapel, and between the stone monoliths, to scan the naked beach.... No one was there.

It was probably some Irish seagulls, pushing off from the black pebbles to gain flight. Or perhaps it was the ghost of the cave hermit, the keeper of the Wee, departing....

The sun had already set and the darkness was dropping around like curtains. I headed to the car, worried about finding my way back to The Seaview Tavern. When I turned around, the chapel and ocean were already shrouded in a gray-black fog layering in from the sea.

My peppered halibut dinner was prepared by the ex-chef of Margaret Thatcher. He had retired to Malin Head years earlier and occasionally cooked the evening meals for the Seaview. Afterward, he liked stopping at their little pub, and he invited me to join him. A group of locals were sitting around on stools singing songs, and a red-faced old man named Pat was playing guitar.

I didn't realize they were taking turns until it landed on me, and suddenly the American had to sing. So I tried an old Irish song I remembered my father singing—"Too-Ra-Loo-Ra-Loo-Ral." Pat joined in on guitar. My tenor voice wasn't too bad, but I couldn't remember all the words, so I repeated the first verse about Killarney. The crowd didn't seem to care; they clapped afterward. I was so relieved I bought them all a round of Guinness.

Directly across from me was a man who hadn't sung yet.

C'mon, Cal, sing your ballad, the bartender demanded. Her name was Breanna.

Yeah, Cal, you know you're going to, so don't make us beg, the chef said.

Cal seemed shy, his soft eyes looking down or away. He was in his mid-thirties, stocky and clean shaven, wearing a tight blue-checkered cowboy shirt. The pleading went on for a while in the Irish way, until he finally sang a long ballad about a lover from the Rosses he lost one day in the fog and storm. By the second verse, he had closed his eyes and began pursing his lips, his body stone still, as if he had shifted into a trance.

When he finished, he got lots of hands on the back, making him smile for the first time, his eyes still not looking at anyone in particular. A minute later, he left to use the bathroom.

That man has a gift, I said to Breanna.

Indeed.

He could have been a fookin' tenor at the Grand Opera in Belfast, Pat added in.

What does he do now? I asked.

Nothing much, Breanna said. He used to do some farm work, then he was on the fishing boats for a while.

Ah, you know, Cal, Pat interrupted, after finishing off the Guinness I had just bought him. Cal's always up to something... getting boat rides back and forth to Scotland. Usually at night. We don't ask....

Ah, be quiet now, Pat, ya drunkin' fool, yelled a tall man from the corner. Don't be talking about what you don't know. Play your guitar again...sing one yourself.

So Pat sang a humorous ballad about some boys of Fairhill. But I wasn't really listening because I was wondering where Cal was. He had left the full pint I had bought for him on the counter. The Guinness foam had disappeared.

What's Cal's last name? I asked, leaning toward the chef.

We just call him Cal.

Could it be McCuade? M-c-C—

Perhaps, Breanna said. He's from Doagh Island, not far from here. His mother, Maggie, was born there, too. But his father, Joe, was from Scotland. So his last name could be spelled the Scottish way—M-a-c-Q-u-a-i-d.

Are his parents still alive?

Been dead a long time, she said. And Cal, he's traveled everywhere—Europe, Africa.... He's older than he looks, you know.

Has he been to the United States?

I wouldn't know about that.

The tall man in the corner broke in again, his voice so loud Pat stopped singing.

That's enough, now, Bree. Cal wouldn't want you talking about him to a stranger.

I can talk to him myself, I said, standing from my stool. Where is he?

Cal won't be coming back.

But he left his beer....

He always does that. Trust me, Cal's gone.

The tall man put on his cap and left, and I drank another Guinness and brooded as the rest of them argued about Cal. One said he often took night boats to Scotland to visit his wife, and that he had married Scottish on purpose to be like his father. Another said he smuggled drugs over to Scotland at night; another said it was black market stuff, not drugs, and that he had been arrested one time but managed to escape to France, which would square with the Garage Wall Man's account of them meeting in Paris.

But I knew they were all just speculating, trying to create a sense of order for everything they don't understand.

Meanwhile, I kept wondering if Cal was the real McCuade, because he was shorter and younger than the Garage Wall Man had let on. And the McCuade I imagined was loud and gregarious, not shy and demure. Unless Cal was just fooling them in the Irish way. But his superb singing voice didn't surprise me, because the real McCuade could do everything well, which made him nearly unreal and metaphysically harder to find.

After a while, I grew tired of their drunken palaver.

What about the Island of Inishtrahull? How do you know he hasn't gone there?

Ah, no one's lived there in over eighty years, an elderly woman in the corner said, waving her cigarette at me.

But what if he did go to Inishtrahull?

Inishtrahull at night? challenged Pat. That's crazy.

What if Inishtrahull is the last place he can go, I said, standing up. The northern limit of his world.... So now I have to go to Inishtrahull, I proclaimed, and downed the last of my Guinness.

You're crazy, Pat repeated, rolling his eyes and then looking for another beer to magically appear on the counter. It's hard enough landing at the north inlet in the daytime. No one could do it at night, certainly not Cal. There are blind rocks around the landing at Portmore, and whirlpools off both the east and west sides of the island.

Maybe not your MacQuaid, but my McCuade could, I fired back. He's much more than a fine voice. In the morning, I will go to Inishtrahull and prove it to you. Breanna, can you get a fisherman to take me there? I will pay whatever the man wants.

They'll be wanting to go around 6:00 a.m., sir, assuming the weather is fine.

Aye, I'll be ready, I said.

I shook her hand.

Thanks for the pint, Pat said.

I nodded and searched around for the chef, but he had already left.

It was 3:00 a.m. before I fell asleep because of Pat's singing and the Malin Head folks laughing right through the floor of my room. But I was still ready on the dock, just down the road from the Tavern, at 6:00 a.m. when the fisherman appeared from the fading darkness in a small trawler. His collar was up and his cap pulled down so it was hard to see his face. When I asked his name, he responded, but I couldn't catch his words. Though I did hear him say, It will be a rough ride, sir. Are ye up for it?

I didn't answer but only raised my hand and pointed in the direction of Inishtrahull. He jerked the boat around and we were enveloped into the gray Irish light, slashing through the rolling swells. It wasn't long before I felt the sickness coming on. But I hadn't thrown up since I was fourteen, so I didn't give in.

Thirty minutes later, a dirty white sky lifted the horizon as we approached Portmore Landing on the north side of the island, the only point of access into Inishtrahull. It was just an inlet between two fissures of rock with a single concrete slab surrounded by corrugated black stone. The fisherman steadied his boat with a long pole while I jumped onto the slab.

I'll be back one hour before dark, he said. Unless the weather turns. Then you'll have to wait until morning. I hope you have some provisions.

I'll be fine. I'll see you this evening…around seven thirty?

One hour before dark, he repeated.

And your name again?

Jeremiah. And you?

McCuade, I said, just to test him.

But he didn't seem to care what my name was and started backing his boat out of the inlet.

Caitlin had packed me two cheese sandwiches, and I had a chocolate bar, two bottles of water, a poncho, my useless flip phone, the flashlight, a penknife, and a pad of paper and pen. I was wearing my heavy coat and my cap.

According to Caitlin, Inishtrahull had been carved out of two-billion-year-old metamorphic rock. The oldest rock in Ireland, she said. The first lighthouse had been built on the eastern hilltop in 1813. I could see the stub of it in the distance and decided to head there first. Behind me, a new automated lighthouse had been built on a hill at the western edge of the island in 1987. Between the two hills was a mile long strip of lowland—a mass of spongy green moss and ancient gray rocks—that I made my way slowly across looking for signs of McCuade.

After a few minutes, I came upon the ruins of a small village, seven one-room stone houses that, according to Caitlin, had been abandoned in the 1920s. The lighthouse keepers stayed until 1987. But now nothing was left on Inishtrahull except for a rare species of silka deer that were so shy and fleet of foot no one ever sees them. And some rats…and McCuade.

The doors of the houses were boarded up, but the windows were all broken free, so it was easy to look inside. Through one of them I saw a pile of blankets next to a decrepit fireplace. I climbed over the sill and into the house. The blankets were dry and crusted from the salt air. *McCuade has been using them.* Under one of the blankets were two paperback books—Shakespeare's *Macbeth* and a collection of poems by Dylan Thomas. Only McCuade would read books about both the Scottish and the Irish, I figured. A pile of white candles sat next to the blankets, but I didn't see any matches. And there was an old wooden chair in the middle of the room.

I was surprised McCuade hadn't been more careful about hiding remnants of himself. *After I explore the rest of the island, I'll come back here to wait for him,* I decided. *Because this is the place.*

I crawled out the window and continued toward the defunct eastern lighthouse. There wasn't any path to follow, so I had to make my own way through the soggy moss and patches of high grass.

The sun disappeared behind some gray-black clouds and the wind picked up. A few minutes later the rain started in, pelting sideways from the east into my face. I pulled down my cap, dropped my head, and continued walking. *If I let the rain bother me, that would mean McCuade is getting inside my mind.* For the first time, though, I felt the pang of aloneness…as if I were the last man walking across the Earth, instead of the last man walking across Inishtrahull.

When I reached the lighthouse, I felt compelled to touch it. The damp gray plaster crumbled into my hand. I looked for Scotland thirty miles across the sea, but couldn't see anything through the rain and low dark clouds. Next to the lighthouse were two derelict buildings shuttered closed. Some old cogs, rusty bits of machinery, and detritus from a disintegrating old fuel tank were scattered about.

There was no place to take cover from the rain. So I pulled on my poncho and sat beneath a doorway, half of my body in the rain. I ate a cheese sandwich and drank some water and tried to imagine the rain letting up and Scotland appearing across the Irish Sea.

Jeremiah won't be coming back in this weather. But that's okay, because I suddenly realized what I should have figured out sooner—McCuade only came to Inishtrahull at night. So I had to spend the night on Inishtrahull to meet him. Even if the weather was fine, I would have to tell Jeremiah to return to Malin Head and come back for me in the morning. And, of course, I would pay him double.

I thought of calling the Seaview to tell Caitlin I was spending the night on the island, but remembered there wasn't any phone coverage on Inishtrahull.

When the rain didn't let up, I headed back to the abandoned house to take shelter. On the way, I detoured to check out Portmore Landing. The tide was up and the waves were rolling through the inlet; impossible conditions for a boat to come in.

At McCuade's house, I took off my poncho and coat and laid them over the back of the chair to dry and covered myself with the blankets to keep warm. It was not yet three in the afternoon; darkness was hours away.

I read a bit of Dylan Thomas, a poem about the green fuse driving the flower, and then I fell asleep through no will of my own.

When I awoke, the rain had stopped and the house was bright with late afternoon sunlight. The wind had ceased, and all of Inishtrahull was quiet, except for a single bird outside the empty window that sounded just like the bird outside Mary Quinn's window...*and Mary Quinn, moonfaced, called on me to get up and move on...to the only place left to go—the western lighthouse....*

I left my coat because it was soaked from the rain and rolled up the poncho and put it in my knapsack with my remaining food and water and the flashlight. By the time I reached the automated lighthouse on the western tip, the sun was getting ready to set over Malin Head. I could see everything so clearly—the bluffs at the tip of Malin Head, the recessed beach where the Wee House was. And Jeremiah in his boat, avoiding the whirlpool off the western shore of the island. He was going to arrive at Portmore one hour before dark, just as he promised. But I wasn't returning with him. I had to wait for McCuade. And I didn't want to run all the way to Portmore to tell him.

North of the island, I could see the half-submerged rocks Caitlin had mentioned and that Jeremiah would find his way through, and Portmore landing itself, clearly visible in the last evening's light.

On a ledge beneath the lighthouse, I sat and ate my second sandwich, saving my chocolate bar for the morning, and kept my eye on Jeremiah so assuredly making his way around the sea rocks. When he reached the inlet, he didn't waste any time waiting for the man who said he was McCuade. He immediately backed his trawler out of the inlet and began his return to the Malin Head pier.

I watched him until the curtains of dusk made it difficult to see, all the while becoming more conscious of the rhythmic flashes of the lighthouse above me. I counted out the strokes—every twenty seconds the light flashed three times, followed by a clicking noise from inside the lighthouse.

I had to decide whether to wait for McCuade at Portmore or back at his house, because it was nearly dark and soon I wouldn't be able to see where I was going without my flashlight, which I wanted to save. The house made more sense, because I might not be able to find my way back to it if I went to Portmore first. Besides, I could smell the rain coming again and needed to be under shelter. McCuade would have to go to the house, too, to spend the night. And I wanted to get to the blankets first.

As I walked through the twilight across the blackened moor, the soggy moss tried to grab my feet, wanting to turn them into ancient Inishtrahull stone.

I had a flash of nervousness—what if Jeremiah didn't come back in the morning and I was abandoned on the island? Then I would have no choice but to rely on the coming of McCuade.

When I could no longer see where I was stepping, I turned on the flashlight.

Hooray for the girl at the Dungloe hardware store! I said aloud.

No one could hear me except for the silka deer.

There was a pile of wood next to the house I hadn't noticed before. After climbing through the window, I found my coat and the two books exactly where I left them. Feeling intensely cold, I got under the blankets and huddled up, hoping that McCuade would come soon and start his nightly fire.

I was afraid to turn off my flashlight, but knew I had to so I could save the battery. When I finally did, the darkness consumed me.

I wished I could light the candles or had some brandy to help pass the night. But McCuade controlled those things.

After drinking half of the water in my second bottle, I leaned my head back against the cold stone wall and listened to the rain that had begun to fall again.

I need to keep track of everything that happens tonight. So I got my pen and pad of paper out of the knapsack and started a log. The problem was writing in the dark, which is difficult to do.

> The rain is falling hard, but the roof is not leaking. The water funnels in through the window and drips onto the stone floor. When the wind stops, I can hear the sea breaking in the distance.

I turned on the flashlight to check my writing. It looked like gibberish.

Who can write in the fookin' dark? I asked aloud with an Irish accent.

But if it looks like gibberish, McCuade won't be able to read it.

I resumed my writing without seeing—

> Rain falling in torrents, then stopping. In the fresh quiet, I can hear tiny footsteps—the silka deer coming to feed on the berries growing in the bushes outside my wall. I want to go out with my flashlight and see them. But they might run away and never come back.
>
> Feeling forlorn. Old Middle English word, forlorn.... A philosopher's word. Heidegger's once. I am forlorn...lost in the world qua world, without Him. And now my world.

I slept for a while. Dreamed I was a priest living atop a hill in a monastery, mingling with the others, but alone. After so many years, questing for it. Finally to be there. And then not having the courage to leave, to admit—this isn't it at all. Because....

After everyone else had left Sister Helen's fifth grade classroom, I remained by the door. Her pale perfect face, her sharp perfect features, ensconced by the severely starched white habit and black veil. I was only ten, but I looked right at her—I love you and want to marry you, I said. When I am older. If you will wait for me, Sister. And she, in her Irish accent, you are a silly boy if you don't know nuns can't marry, except to Jesus. She showed me her silver ring and told me about the church's desperate need for vocations. If you have enough love for God, she said, you could be His emissary, His blood in life, His priest. Oh yes, I said, then as a priest I will marry you. And she—priests and nuns can't marry either, my sweet boy. But, Sister, in the Church of Jesus Magdalene in France, they can. There is no church such as that, she replied with impatience. There is, I said. A man sleeping behind the rectory told me so. And he looked just like a saint, Sister. Just like a saint. A hobo sleeping behind the rectory? she asked, shocked. That's impossible. But I saw him, Sister. And that means we could live in France, Sister. If you will wait for me....

McCuade whispered from outside the house—I've been here since you entered Donegal. But I could feel his presence inside.

I climbed out the window with my flashlight. But there was only the dark wind and slicing rain.

Because I am forlorn, I am hearing him before he has arrived.

I went back into the house and ate the chocolate bar and finished my water. There was nothing left.

McCuade might bring water. But he has already left the blankets, and maybe that is enough.

I closed my eyes again, but opened them a minute later, startled by the stillness. The rain and wind had ceased. I returned to my log—

> What a fool I am for not figuring out sooner what I must have known for quite a while—McCuade is more than a man.... He is the essence of all one imagines McCuade to be...the essence of something we call McCuade.

I will be okay until morning.... But I must stay awake because he will come before dawn. And Jeremiah will arrive just after dawn and won't wait more than a moment at Portmore Landing.

Portmore...the sea rock flesh of it. The truth into Inishtrahull and the truth out of it. And Jeremiah, my Saint Christopher, will carry me from Inishtrahull to Malin Head, from the two-billion-year-old McCuade rock to....

Because he has seen me and knows I am not equipped to stay longer.

The rain started up again, for the final time, so loud I couldn't hear anything except his low humming voice inside the raw dampness of the house...ancient white noise that only I was attuned to recognize. Like at the Dungloe slipway, hearing the primal Pythagorean chord....

I am ready, I wanted to say aloud.

WHAT WAS THAT? Nietzsche asked about the corporeal life of Jesus. And the apostles, after Jesus's death, wondering—WHO WAS THAT?

The rain had receded forever so that I could hear his footsteps on the green-soaked moss just beyond the door.

McCuade, is that you? I yelled across the darkness.

I turned on my flashlight and climbed out the window, this time determined to see what was there. I walked through the damp high grass around the cottage but couldn't find him.

Could he have gone inside the house while I was looking for him outside? So I went back toward the window, and that's when I heard him calling from inside his stone house—McCuade, is that you?

He is calling himself now. How cunning of him.

Though the rain had stopped, I was still damp to the bone. So I went back inside and wrapped myself in the blankets again and took out my notepad. McCuade was one step ahead, so I needed to keep writing down everything and make a plan.

> All quiet now. Would love some water.

Strawberries, she said. He brought me—

> Passed an old cistern between Portmore Landing and McCuade's house, but I'm sure the water inside is bacteria ridden.

Nearly 3:00 a.m. Heard a noise in the corner. One of the rats. Put my flashlight on to look for him, but they are too quick to see. No more sitting on the ground, I decided, not with the rat moving about. So I sat on the chair, my damp coat still hanging off the back of it, and wrapped the blankets around my legs. I must look like a vagrant. What the hell has happened to me?

A slight sound on the outside of the door. Scratchy, like tiny claws. If someone wants in, they should just use the empty window. I reluctantly put my flashlight on and stuck my head out the window again.

Is anyone there?

I waited.

Damn this!

But the "damn this" came at me from behind. He was in the house somewhere. I shined the flashlight around. Nothing in the room but the chair, the old fireplace, the two books and candles, and broken pieces of a wooden table in the corner.

Decided to go outside one final time. Slight breeze. Nothing else but the northern Irish silence. Smell of the sea and passing rain and mossy greenness. Could nourish one for a while. Better than.... Kept my eye on the window as I paced before the front of the house. Heard something moving inside. A dragging sound across the stone floor. Poked my flashlight through the window. Nothing.

Who the hell is there?

The echo of the words resounded behind me.

Feeling angry for the first time and sick of whatever he is up to.... And hungry, and thirsty. Feeling...at my end.

Everything in the house was exactly as I left it. Must have been the rat, I decided. McCuade is probably on his way. His boat delayed by the storm.

All is calm now, so he should be coming.

Just to test him, I stuck my head out the window and yelled—McCuade! Then retreated inside to see if I would hear my own voice again calling him, or calling myself. But there was nothing.

> Conclusion: you can't make yourself hear McCuade. He has to do the calling and we have to be ready to listen. And that's why everyone except McCuade has left Inishtrahull. And that's why on Inishtrahull, Ireland's northern-most island, time loops around like the beam from the lighthouse. Things seem to happen, with some variation, and time passes. But there is no real movement beyond the inside and outside voices, and one is trapped within an unresolved moment. The magnetic opposite of what happens five miles across the sea at the Wee House, where one tries to hold on to a moment that seems forever fleeting, while gazing through the twin pillars at the twilight sea and the dreamy island of Inishtrahull, feeling the texture of time itself passing like shadows from a distant planet.

I have to leave this house and go down to Portmore to free myself from this moment. McCuade will have to bring his boat in there, and Jeremiah, too, sometime after dawn. And I will be waiting.

The rain was over, and I figured it wouldn't be any colder at Portmore than inside McCuade's stone house.

There was still some power left in the flashlight, so I decided to keep it on until the vague light appeared on the horizon.

I took the Dylan Thomas book and left Macbeth. Packed up my pad of paper and my empty water bottles because I didn't want to litter on Inishtrahull. And took one of the blankets, which seemed fair, leaving the other for McCuade.

I'm taking off now, McCuade, I said in a low voice like I really didn't want him to hear, before climbing out the window for the last time.

I stepped into the high grass and waited to hear his tenor voice repeating my words from inside the house. But there was nothing.

The hell with you. Afraid to say the words aloud. And unsure whether they were meant for him or for me.

Tears welled in my eyes. *It's just exhaustion. Or perhaps wistfulness over a failed idea.*

Something crawled across my cheek. A spider? I brushed my hands across my face, put on my wet coat, and then draped the blanket over my shoulders and walked with determination through the soggy moss, flashlight aimed at my feet, and every twenty seconds the beam from the lighthouse displaying my path ahead.

Afraid to hear his voice behind me, I sang "Too-Ra-Loo-Ra-Loo-Ral," just like I had at the pub.

> Complete darkness at Portmore Landing. No stars, no moon. The clouds are invisible. The sky has retreated. 4:30 a.m.

There was a tiny boathouse next to the concrete dock that I missed seeing when I landed. Its green wooden door was padlocked and there was no other way inside. So I sat on the metamorphic rock next to it, resting my back against my knapsack and covering myself with the blanket.

> Broke my own pledge and turned the flashlight off. Who cares? Sunrise will come in less than an hour.
>
> Closed my eyes and counted the seconds between the sweeping flashes from the lighthouse a half mile away.

I wanted to sleep but wouldn't let myself. Without warning, the rain started again, falling hard this time. *McCuade wants me to return to his stone hovel.* But I put my poncho on over the blanket, drew down my Irish cap, and huddled against the door of the boathouse. I worried Jeremiah might not come because of the rain. And that dawn, itself…might not arrive.

My pants were soaked. So I put on the flashlight to see if I was sitting in a puddle. The beam was already dimming so I turned it off. Thought about throwing the flashlight into the sea, but didn't.

The rain was so constant, the darkness so fixed, I wondered if I was still caught inside the looping Inishtrahull moment, even though I was no longer inside his house.

Total impasse.

Where are you, McCuade? I yelled, no longer fearing my own words coming back at me through him.

I fixed my eyes toward the east, past the low rocky hill where the abandoned lighthouse stood, and challenged the dawn light to appear, and challenged myself not to stop staring till it did.

Waves of darkness seemed to be closing around my huddled pose upon the rain-drenched concrete slab—the last small stage inside a disintegrating theater….

I looked away just long enough to cut the top off of one of the plastic water bottles with my penknife. Then placed the makeshift cup out in the rain. *I am freezing and wet, but I don't have to die of thirst.*

Whenever the lighthouse beam flashed, I checked to see if there was enough water worth drinking. And that's how I missed the gray-green light coming over the peak of the hill and leaking around the sides of the brightening sea.

The rain slowed to a drizzle and I could hear, beyond the final storm, a dog barking somewhere, but knew that was impossible.

A few minutes later, the throaty sound of a boat engine not far off. I turned west to see a bow light closing in on Portmore Landing.

It had to be Jeremiah. Except that he wouldn't leave Malin Head until after first light. And the dawn was not yet full. And he didn't have a dog with him before.

As the approaching light neared the inlet, I could see the outline of the boat but wasn't sure if it was Jeremiah's.

Jeremiah! Is that you? McCuade! Is that you? Jeremiah! McCuade!

Yes. It is.

Chapter Six

THE LORD

I

The lord lived in his castle on the northern reaches of Ireland. Though some believed his castle was in the west of Scotland. Others weren't sure. But they all knew who he was, and that he lived alone.

II

When the castle had to be sold, like so many others, because the bills could no longer be paid, the lord was forced to turn it into a museum. The museum trustees required, however, that the lord remain living in the castle, because then the public would be more inclined to visit. The trustees further required that the public be able to view all of the rooms, including the lord's living quarters, because this would allow them a glimpse of the lord himself, thus making the lord's castle a museum experience beyond all others.

And the lord would never be allowed to leave his castle, a condition the trustees deemed fair since the lord would live for free, in perpetuity, inside his grand ancestral home. In return, the public would always know exactly where the lord was.

After a while, the lord lost the aura of his munificence and the people referred to him derisively as the lord-man who was lucky enough to live inside a castle.

III

The four pints of Guinness were lined up on the old wooden bar waiting for him, and he had his usual forty minutes, ten for each pint, which was not a problem if no one talked to him. But someone always did, because what kind of man drinks in such a manic fashion, enslaved to the clock?

If you want to get drunk quickly, why not take some shots?

You will have a hellava piss after four pints!

Could make a man sick, even if he is Irish.

Ah, let him go, laddy. It's a bit of a miracle, you know… drinking four of God's pints in such a wee bit of time.

What's the man's name?

He doesn't have time to talk, so he won't say.

He looks a bit like the lord himself. Probably thinks he's too good to talk to us.

No, yea gits…he's just the man who works for the lord, coming out to drink a few….

Eyes down, the lord-man used his nondrinking hand to feel the texture at the edge of the dark wooden bar. He imagined the splintered grooves as keys to an ancient instrument from inside the Earth that he, like a god, was playing…a song beyond all human hearing, until he was not at St. George's Tavern anymore, but beyond the shape of himself, beyond the shape of a creature who eats and defecates, and beyond the curious people who observe him but do not know him.

By the third pint, his drinking hand shook, and he worried about the two museum guards already finishing their late-night dinner, urinating against the castle wall, and returning to their rounds. They would check all forty-four castle doors that had been built and measured by a being who never quite understood the full dimensions of the lord.

Over time, the crowds at the tavern increased, because people wanted to witness the lord-man's drinking. And he would have difficulty swallowing with so many watching. Still, he persevered…. Always out of the tavern by 10:50 p.m., dodging in and out of the dark alleys to lose those trying to follow him to prove they knew who he was, which made it more difficult for him to get back through the window by 11:00 p.m.

The guards checked only the doors and not the windows, but they would come into his chambers a few minutes after eleven to see him in the flesh.

IV

One night, the lord barely reached the castle in time. In a nervous rush, he withdrew the rope, which he kept inside his coat, threw it over the tree limb, and ascended to his window. Once on the sill, he looked back, as he always did, to make sure the guards had not seen him, and that's when he noticed a dark shape at the base of the oak tree. He worried that it could be someone from town spying on him. So he waited for the guard to pass on his rounds, then rappelled back down the wall.

The shape was a body bundled in a fetal position beneath a dark blanket. When he touched the person, a mass of long black hair appeared and a woman's voice spoke to him.

Please…let me stay, she whispered. I am too tired to move.

You can come inside if you wish, but you have to climb the rope.

She didn't answer. Her hair retreated.

You can stay here, of course. The guards probably won't see you if you remain under the blanket. But you will have to leave with the first light. Here is twenty pounds. Use it to come inside the castle when it opens at ten. When you reach my chambers on the tour, cough a few times and I will know it is you. And I will help you…. All right?

She didn't answer but reached out a hand to take the bank note, which the lord interpreted as a yes.

All night he looked out the window to keep watch on her shape under the oak tree. Just before dawn, he fell asleep in his chair wearing his father's purple silk robe.

When he awoke, her shape was gone.

The lord doubted himself.... Had he really seen a dark-haired woman under the tree or was she a dream resulting from four rushed pints of Guinness? Either way, he was sure he would never see her again. And if she used the twenty pounds to spend on herself, so be it.

Still, the lord found himself listening for her cough. Sometimes imagining it inside a particular woman's voice from the gallery, making his nerves twang. Since he hadn't seen her face, he imagined every woman with long dark hair to be the woman from under the tree, whimsically believing she was his destiny. How else can you explain the uncanniness of her sleeping beneath his window?

Weeks passed, and he gave up on seeing her. He longed to disappear as well...but knew he couldn't because of the contract. Except by death.

So he began applying makeup to his face. The lord found the old white makeup on his mother's bathroom shelf. He also stopped dressing in his day clothes and wore his purple robe all the time, except when he went to the tavern. At first he worried the trustees might think he was violating the appearance terms of the agreement, but evidently they liked the idea of the lord being decadently regal.

Once the woman came to him in a dream. Still he couldn't see her face because she remained under her blanket with her dark hair spread on the gray lawn and one hand cupped upward as if waiting to receive a coin from god.

Maybe that was enough—seeing the underside of her hand... smallish and smooth, like a girl's hand. Standing behind her, he commanded—arise and walk!

And she did, but with her back to him so he still couldn't see her.

Eventually, he used up all of his mother's white makeup. He could have asked for more with his weekly procurement order, but it wouldn't be the same...with the touch of his mother's swollen fingers still inside the old jar. He had worn the last remnants of her...she, who would have been repulsed by his decision to become a prisoner in his own castle. You are nothing more than a clown-lord, she would say. She, who was lost to him now. And father, too, lost long ago.

V

He was sitting on the floor with his back against the bed, eyes closed, and his head dropped to the side, when the first line of tourists filed by his bedroom doorway a little after 10:00 a.m. Since he couldn't erase his face, the lord decided to negate his presence by posing in death mode. No matter the reason…murdered, accidentally drowned in the stream…. *Let them create their own stories.*

After staring at the dead-lord in frozen wonder, their eyes touched on all his things, now given over to them—his gold nail clippers, the polished silver hand mirror, his father's old shaving bowl that he pretended to still use, and the family pistol from the 1870s….

Every day he was the dead-lord again, only in a different position. Perhaps with his bare legs splayed wide from out of his purple robe and wearing no underwear.

His eyes were usually closed, with just a bit of tongue showing between his dry lips. No water or moving until noon, when the museum closed for lunch and he could muck about for an hour, have a piss…. Then back at it.

The lord was excited that his bedroom had become a stage and that all his possessions were props. Living as a prisoner didn't bother him as much, because his imagination was free to work his death art. It's a hell of a thing, he muttered to himself.

Every day he expected the trustees to shut down his theater. By contract, though, he was staying in his rooms and, by contract, the visitors were still viewing him.

But the sporadic lines of voyeurs soon turned into crowds jamming the doorway to witness his static death poses. Tickets were sold in advance. Some of the visitors were theater lovers, some tabloid junkies, some believers in death art, and some interested in the lord's new revelationary symbolism.

The trustees were beside themselves. This was no longer a castle museum where one had the unusual opportunity to witness the lord. It was royal improv, and they were proud to take ownership of it, as if this was their plan all along.

In this way, the lord achieved notoriety through both of his manifestations: as the lord-man at St. George's Tavern, and as the dead-lord inside the castle walls. And his dual presence would continue until someone figured out they were the same being.

The lord himself didn't fully understand either of his roles, except as metaphor. During his drinking quest at the tavern, he believed he represented all men; posing as the dead-lord he represented a higher truth that folks must have known for a long time but were hesitant to acknowledge—their lord was dying.

One day, he posed with eyes open, a mistake because he needed to blink. With one of his father's ties winched tightly around his bare neck, he pretended to have been hung. All was fine until he became distracted by a blue thread hanging from the back of his mother's oriental chair that he had moved into his room. By death choice, he had to stare at the chair for nearly two hours, until the pattern of blue and green lilies inside the chair intoxicated him….

When he was a boy, his mother used to point out the water lilies as they walked past the castle stream—No one should ever disturb them, she said, because they are the most delicate of all things.

When noon arrived, he yanked out the loose thread and then worried about the line of weakness running down the back of the chair. His body shook from not eating and being frozen in position for too long.

He remembered his mother sitting and reading in the chair before going to bed. Her lumbar cushion was still in place. He could smell her if he got close enough. Not her, but the way she used to smell.

He took the cushion, used it as a pillow, stretched out on the carpet and closed his eyes…. And she was standing over him. And he, as a boy, was waving goodbye…moving only his hand—

I'm going outside now, Mother.... And his mother never responding, because she knew he would return. So she never waited for him.

His father in his study, not knowing when anyone left or arrived, until he drowned in the castle stream. Not by accident, but because his father never learned to swim. His body disappearing under the water lilies that his mother refused to disturb to recover him.

And that's when the boy-lord began to swim at secret times, teaching himself and telling no one...the castle stream cold and recessive. Swimming not to look for his father, but to get past him, who lay in the primal mud and darkness beneath the brown reeds and forbidden lilies.

Decades later, the lord once again swam in the castle stream, by additional codicil agreement with the trustees. It was the only time he could leave the castle. But it had to be at dusk when no one would see him. Because people needed to believe the lord was always at home.

In winter, dusk came on as soon as the castle museum closed. And the lord would make his way down the path of crushed cedar chips and pine needles carrying his towel, the guard close behind. After a while, he no longer wore his bathing suit. The guard said nothing as the lord made his way in complete nakedness. Eventually, the lord left the towel behind as well.

By January, the water was covered with a thin layer of blue ice that he broke apart with his bare feet and elbows, his translucent skin vaguely visible in the silver twilight.

The lord noticed that the water in the stream was gradually becoming brackish, even though the sea was two miles away. The lord told no one. Secretly, he thought of himself as the salt-lord.

Sometimes he would swim under the ice and then return to the black watery surface. If the guard saw him, he didn't seem to care. The lilies were still there...preserved inside gray globes of ice floating a foot below the surface. No one knew about them except the lord, who rubbed his shoulder and ribs against the ice globes in the freezing darkness, touching the one thing his mother had forbidden him to touch, while never touching the lily itself. And telling no one because he talked to no one. So people continued to assume that water lilies simply died away in winter, because it made sense to them from their world above. As did the story of a lord who would always be present inside the castle so they could always know who they were in relation to him. And if they needed stories of the lord, he gave them with his death art, which helped to explain the mysteries of their world.

Every time the lord swam that winter, he was able to stay under the ice a bit longer, and the guards never noticed that either. Or how afterward, on his way back to the castle, the lord no longer shivered, because the great cold was making him stronger.

Sometimes, walking naked up the path in the chilled night air, the lord felt like a god.

VI

On the floor, with his head on his mother's cushion, the dying-lord turned into the napping-lord. He never moved an inch, nor did he eat or use the bathroom.

After a few days, for no certain reason, he moved from the floor to the bed. Shortly after that he went under the covers and became the sleeping-lord. Finally—the naked-sleeping-lord atop the bed without covers, his thinning body curled and his back to the visitors who were increasing in number.

He still escaped at night for his one-hour quest to the pub as the lord-man, the four pints of Guinness becoming his only sustenance. But he no longer needed to urinate after drinking them. And it became harder to climb the rope back up to his room, and exhausting to remove his clothes and throw his concave body onto the bed. During the day, it became easier to remain curled in one position, making him wonder if he had already died and didn't know it.

All that was left for him was to turn the other way, face them with his nakedness.

One of the guards began to feel sorry for him and entered the room late at night to cover the lord's body with the bedspread. In the morning, though, the lord was again uncovered. And that's how the people believed he would always be, except that it was hard not to notice how emaciated he had become. Some questioned if the spectacle was still death art or if the lord was actually dying.

He could see himself through the two mirrors in his bedroom—the one above his dresser reflecting across to the one on the wall by the door, and then to his white buttocks that, surprisingly, still had some flesh on it. Seeing himself as they did, he could imagine what it was like to be them.

But they did not understand what they were witnessing. They believed that the lord would rise up at the end of the museum day...get dressed, eat potted herrings while reading newspapers, drink red wine and smoke cigars with Mozart on the record player, write letters from his desk using a fountain pen with the royal insignia... mailing them without addresses. Some people in town claimed they had received such a letter, though no one had actually seen one.

No one complained about the lord being naked, not even the trustees. Because how rare a thing—to see the lord in his purity, and how good for the museum's business. And no one dared proclaim voyeurism either.

VII

Remain posed...let the thoughts dull themselves until they escape diagonally, toward the northern sea...

...from beyond the sad empty rooms, I appear, unfolding in silence....

...Who are these people?... Is it not enough to be outside of me, they want inside, too?...Or above, staring down at me...

...when I open my eyes, I see them without their knowing...their unclean hands and mouths, through mirrors, until the end of their days....

…How I despise their desire to see me change, so they can possess another image of the lord…who understands less than they believe…their debilitating fear of mortality…and who is too weak to continue being their spirit through flesh, their tongue through fire…and a way to depart not yet revealed….

…I'm still here, Mother, with almost nothing left, except one more moment, always one more moment, not yet theirs…that they, in time, will claim as their own, making them believe they are one step closer to eternity….

…I walk up the path to a castle built by rough hands, and with imperfect understanding…with nothing to warm me because great cold breeds strength…and always careful not to touch the most fragile filaments of Earth's beauty….

…Entering in darkness once more, like no one else…until a white flash of mind through stale smoke, and a new beginning…

…no one else at home, and home no longer mine…

…wanting to say what they cannot hear—there is nothing more I can do for you, nothing more you can do to me…

…desiring to finish it then, without words, even though they will always believe it is not yet time….

Who is it who said what I just heard?

VIII

There is a cough at the door. The lord turns his nakedness toward her. The other faces do not exist.

The dark hair from the spreading lawn. Black eyes. Face thin like his, and ageless. Her shoulders slightly slumped beneath her black shawl.

When she coughs again, he has no doubt.

The tour group is excited because they have seen the lord move.

He stands naked, facing them like a risen sick god.

As he steps toward the doorway, they are moved away by the guides to make room for the next group of witnesses. She lingers behind unnoticed, leaning on the doorjamb because she can no longer stand on her own.

The lord takes her hand. She whispers her name so faintly, the sound almost undetectable…Ashra.

She follows him. Bare feet shuffling across the planked floor toward the room with the white marble tub, the only place the guards never check.

Ashra sits upon a bed of towels he has mounded together for her.

When the next group arrives, the lord, for the first time, seems unaware of their presence. His final manifestation will not be a manifestation at all but simply living for the lost idea of his own being, rather than for them. They will not understand. If they did, they would call him the true-lord.... Without their knowing, he is the last-lord.

The time of discernable death art is over. The lord pulls on loose pants, tightening them as much as he can on his concave waist, and then one of his too-large white shirts. No one will see him naked again, except her.

Feeling hunger as if for the first time, the lord sends a message down to the kitchen. He orders enough food for a family—large portions of soup and bread and sausages and cheese…apples and figs, lemon pie, milk, red wine, and even some potted herring. By contract, the lord has the right to eat and drink as much as he wants, and they must serve him.

All day the lord eats…his shrunken stomach not even a memory. The audiences come and go. Every so often the lord stands, takes his plate of food into the bathroom, and comes back with it nearly empty. The viewers chock this up to a royal idiosyncrasy. In this way, Ashra eats as well, renewing her strength. And the lord and she stare at each other as if seeing, for the first time, the other part of themselves.

Eventually, some man from the crowd yells out, even though absolute silence is required during the tour—Ah, look at him now. He's nothing but a bloody eating-lord. He's just like us.

That evening, the lord skips his swim at dusk. The guards say nothing about the aberration, but the lord can sense their suspicions. After filling up the ancient marble bathtub for Ashra, he decides it best to continue his routines and steals out the window for St. George's Tavern. Once there, he can feel the people looking at him differently, as if they know he is not the same being.

When the lord cannot finish his second pint, because he no longer believes in drinking just to confirm their idea of who he is, the pub crowd becomes restless. He senses they are about to turn on him, so he leaves early, vowing to never return.

Several men follow him. The lord does not have the strength to elude them all. Still, he moves faster, sweating into his shirt as he ducks into shadows and turns down narrow lanes.

He loses them all except for one. But there is no more time. At the castle, he throws his rope over the tree limb and begins his ascent. The last man sees him and betrays him—I know who you are, he yells. I will tell everyone it was the lord himself who was afraid to drink with us.

In that moment, the lord-man ceased to exist, just as the dead-lord had ceased to exist.

After the guard checks on him at 11:00 p.m., the lord strips off his shirt and pants and curls up with Ashra in the marble tub. He turns on the hot water and lets it run.

Ashra talks about her girlhood in Scotland, and later living in Russia. About how she had a son who was stolen from her shortly after his birth. She has been searching for him ever since…across Europe and, finally, to Donegal.

She tells him she has no memory of sleeping under the lord's oak tree. And the lord says that it doesn't matter.

We will look for your son, he says.

That night, the lord sleeps on his bed and Ashra on a pile of shirts and towels. But before dawn, the lord joins her. And, without exchanging words, they become one.

Afterward, he whispers—Can you swim?

I learned as a girl…across Loch Lomond.

The water was cold?

Oh, yes.

She tucks her head under his chin and falls back asleep.

IX

In the morning, the lord brings her some breakfast and they both put on clean white shirts. They could have continued on, happy as two birds in a stone cage, if not for the betrayal.

At dusk, the lord heads down to the stream for his swim and Ashra throws a dark blanket out the window and climbs naked down the rope. She waits until dark, covering herself with the blanket, then walks in secret to the stream. The lord swims longer than usual, waiting for her. The guard says nothing.

Upstream, Ashra slips quietly into the water. The guard hears nothing until she begins to swim.

What, ho! Is that you over there, sir? I can't see you.

Ashra reaches him and the lord holds her tight.

Yes, I'm right here, the lord answers. I'll be coming out soon.

Okay, because it's getting dark, sir.

A group of men gather at the castle under the lord's window. They see the rope still hanging there and one of them starts to climb. Another one yells—Come out here! Or are you too good to drink with us, you crazy old loon?

The guard at the castle calls for help, and the guard at the stream begins to run up the path crying out to the lord—I'll be back for you in a minute, sir.

But the lord is already gone, under the ice with Ashra, both holding their breath as long as they can, their white bodies brushing against the globed water lilies that disintegrate at their touch because the water has warmed in recent days. For the first time, the lord feels the lilies with his hand, and then his chest, and then his groin.

The lord and Ashra come up for air easily through the eggshell ice and go back under again. As they round the bend, the ice disappears completely and they swim freely. In two miles, they will reach the Irish sea.

X

Everyone heard about the men breaking into the castle, and the rumors that the lord himself had been drinking at the pub.

And everyone continued to believe they had the right to see the lord. When he was not visible in his rooms at the castle, they told themselves he would be there the next day. Thus, visiting the castle became a gamble with time, something they understood.

The lord is always inside his castle and will never leave, the museum guides tell the crowds.

In line, people talk about their hope of seeing the lord eating, or sleeping, or perhaps in one of his death poses.

Eventually, doubt sets in.... Maybe the man they saw wasn't really the lord. Maybe no one has seen the lord.

Chapter Seven
PRAXILLA

I

When I called out, you would come to me…to Praxilla of Sicyon, courtesan and poet…who, by the will of Aphrodite, would soon be forgotten. Yet I was always there with you, through all the storied moments of your lives.

Come to me now…let me touch your nearly divine and burning flesh. Remembering…when you were once drained of life, the black Dionysian sickness consuming even your bones, you implored—Help me, Praxilla, I feel a weakness coming on I haven't known before…a draining of passion…my power to love nothing more than a sick man's dream. Death will arrive, and this time I will not have the strength to evolve through the seasons. Take me to Asclepius; only he can cure me.

So I transported you in my wooden cart to the great god of health, Asclepius, and his daughter, Hygeia, and told them about Dionysus's curse despoiling your flesh into vapor, because your hunting dogs had chased his maenads into the sea. And after whispering to me, Asclepius ordered me to carry you to the Caucasus Mountains. So I bore your diminishing body upon my shoulders into the shadow of Mount Elbrus, where we clung deathless beneath the cliffs sacred to the fathergod, and from the darkened rocks you tasted the thick black excretion no one but Asclepius has ever known.

In that graying moment, you regained the original spark the fathergod granted you when the king of Cyprus cleaved the myrrh tree in half and your nascent flesh issued from the essence of the earth into the timeless present. And I, Praxilla, vowed to love you and watch over you...all of my days.

Come to me now. Come to the poet who first gave words to your deathless voice, spoken as you departed into the undergloom with the hollow-eyed spirits crowding around, demanding to know what you would miss most from the bright green world as it frittered away in an amorphous and darkening wake behind you—

Loveliest of what I leave behind is the sunlight, and loveliest after that the shining stars, and the moon's face, but also cucumbers that are ripe, and pears, and apples....

II

Your story has been told, about Ares sending his wild boar to gore you with its tusk. And the great god of war watching as you bled to death in agony. Because Ares feared that Aphrodite might love you more than him.

But that story is not complete. Someone else was there...Praxilla of Sicyon. Her story of self-sacrifice long forgotten. Persephone and Aphrodite saw to that.

Aphrodite warned you not to hunt. But you continued roaming the forest on the southern slope of Mount Lykaion, where Rhea gave birth to Zeus and created the sacred source of the Neda River, until your dogs came across the wild boar. You threw your spear and wounded it, but the boar removed the spear from his snout and chased you through the thick trees until Praxilla intervened and threw herself before the boar, which gouged her breast with his tusk.

As Praxilla lay bleeding, there was time for Aphrodite to arrive in her chariot drawn by a team of wild blue doves. She begged you to come with her and save yourself. But you would not leave Praxilla. The boar charged again and gored you in the groin. From the air, Aphrodite watched you slowly die, then she came down and held you in her arms. As your blood fell to the ground, red anemone flowers sprang from the earth. And from Aphrodite's tears, the white rose was born, which reddened with her blood when Aphrodite pricked herself on a thorn as she shuddered to hold you more tightly.

I died in the same moment as you. Together, our exanimate souls arrived in the underworld. Persephone was thrilled to have you again. For she had been in love with you since Aphrodite entrusted you to her when you were an infant. And when you grew into a beautiful young man, Persephone became your lover. Madly jealous, Aphrodite restored you to the green world so she alone could possess you.

Aphrodite…the source of all your troubles even before you came into existence….

Offended by the Queen of Cyprus for claiming that her daughter, Myrrha, was more beautiful than Aphrodite, the goddess of love infected Myrrha with incestuous love for her own father, the king…. And Myrrha contrived a union at night when her father was lost in drunkenness. Finding out later that he had violated and impregnated his own daughter, the king flew into a rage and raised his ax against Myrrha. To save her, Aphrodite turned Myrrha into a myrrh tree and the king cleaved the tree instead…and you were born from that tree.

To ensure that the king would never find you, Aphrodite entrusted your infant body to the care of Persephone. And when you became a young man, Persephone loved you….

After our slaying by the boar, Persephone was thrilled to repossess you. But she would not admit Praxilla into the underworld. Because sanctioning her death would mean that Praxilla loved you more than Persephone did.

Praxilla's eyes were heavy with the burden of death when Persephone spoke to her—*Your reward, Praxilla, is that you will never be forgotten. You will forever be the only mortal woman who passed into the underworld and rose to live again. Only you, Praxilla….*

But that would never come to pass. Aphrodite cursed the memory of Praxilla into oblivion. And Praxilla didn't care…she only desired to be with you, while her soul already faded upward into the brightening twilight.

In a slant of seconds, Persephone paled into nothingness and Asclepius breathed upon her. Do with me as you will, Praxilla whispered to him, not opening her eyes. So she suffered the tortuous pains of becoming mortal again, and the touch of his rough hands…lifting her upon his shoulder, and the journey to Mount Elbrus where she drank the sacred black excretion from the darkening rocks of the Caucasus. The rent in her breast repaired itself and Praxilla was restored to life inside the fragmented green world where no one would ever know of her sacrifice for you, or that her sacrifice allowed Aphrodite the time to arrive in her chariot, witness the boar's attack upon her lover, and hold his expiring body in her arms.

After Praxilla's restoration, Aphrodite was consumed with spreading the greatness of your story. She entered the mind of Sappho, the greatest poet of the Hellenes, urging her to teach young girls every spring to mourn for you so intensely that their souls nearly fractured…and the women of Athens to tear their tunics and beat their breasts until they bled for you, franticly crying out for you to live again, their frenzied passion a welcome alternative to the passive role of women during the festivals of Demeter, and their only chance to experience unbridled emotion amidst the tyranny over their lives in Athens, with the endless phallic war against the Lacedaemon….

And Aphrodite taught the women of Cyprus to create house-top gardens with anemone seeds planted in shallow soil so that the flowers would spring up and quickly die, followed by the singing of dirges and ceremonial wailing over an effigy of a beautiful dying boy….

III

Finally, you came to me in the lotus-smelling dark, pressing upon my thighs inside a swirling smoke of myrrh and frankincense.

My gown disappearing by your will, and the covered divan as well, until there was nothing.... Spreading myself by your will until my own widening darkness edged me backward into a divine graying light—the luminous margin where near-gods mingle with mortal flesh—my weakening hands drifting across your hips and shoulders, my closed eyes seeing without seeing, but sensing your cutaneous breath upon me—tongues of fire across my paling skin, amidst the rising odor of onycha, the forbidden incense of the gods....

Waiting until just before...remembering with mortal regret what Asclepius had whispered, cursing his words and at the same time hoping they were true...*he must desire a woman who at the final moment rejects him, in order to live again*...blind sensing to recognize the moment just before the moment...suspended by the uplifting drafts of the gods' bright shadows, balanced between the heaven-arching abyss and the vanishing Earth below...your hand unfurling my hair while feeling the surge of you, the surge of all gods who, in divine madness, desire to enter human flesh...to enter Praxilla, born from a father who was not a god, yet loved by a man who was birthed by the fathergod...paling deeper into a fading plane of eternal twilight, toward the crushing moment, the breach of it—flashing with madness into the divine libidinous luminosity.

Be gone from me! I cried, and in that same instant, I was back on my divan, unclothed, retreating from my nakedness...and you, withdrawing into the margins of the visible, with rigid-shifting limbs and a final glancing back, before your eyes closed and your flesh turned marmoreal, like you seemed to have always been....

Lamenting, I cried out for you to return...for a man greater than any god because you can do what no god can—die and live again...born, as you were, from nature's sacred core. And even though the gods, with their Earth-tilting powers, would continue to savage you, you would forever exist beyond their compass of time and the limits of their coveted physical world. And that is why I, Praxilla, poet and courtesan, have believed in you more than any god...contumaciously knowing that, in my moment of rejecting you, I would somehow get you back. Because a courtesan who says no is nothing, and a poet who says no is nothing. But a poet-courtesan who says no can sacrifice herself triumphant.

So I lie upon my divan waiting for you...I, Praxilla, the truth shaper...even though my poetry would be forgotten, my chance for immortality lost, by curse of Aphrodite, the goddess of lies.

Praxilla, who seemed to be two women to the men of Athens—courtesan at their wine and lemon flower symposiums, and the poet teaching choral songs to the young girls. Praxilla, who really is one woman, one being....

Girl of the lovely glance, looking out through the window, your face is virgin, lower down you are a married woman.

How many times have I cried out for you while staring beyond the horizon and the fading golden wheels of the sun? My tears, red as blood, falling on stony ground where roses would later bloom....

And if the entire world were offered to me in a golden bowl, I would trade it for one moment's touch from you....

Come to me now, possess me fully with your reborn passion... penetrate my body and limbs until only Thanatos awaits...and Persephone who, with shocked eyes, casts me out once more from her underground kingdom.

Come to me...melt my mind into fervid flesh, ravish me until Praxilla of Sicyon is no more...Praxilla, who carried you to Asclepius and followed his every word, redeeming you into life, so you could possess me with your terrible and timeless eros.... Take me beyond this world of excruciating sunrise seconds.... Come, my lover...my man-god...my lord...my Adonis.

Chapter Eight

HERACLITUS

I

Most of the rocks hit my back and my arms as I was walking away. Except for the first one, which hit my forehead. *That will leave a mark. But the next time I am at the Olympiad, they will see the mark and remember who I am.*

Except that I will never return to this site along the Alpheus River. Not because of the stoning, but because it is their Olympiad, not mine. They are so proud of their wrestling and running and discus throwing, and especially their glorious chariot races. And after a man wins, he receives honor and gifts from the city. But he does not deserve it as much as I do. Because I know about the Logos, and he does not. And when I try and teach them about the Logos, they do not listen. For they are happy in their life of darkness.

The great thinker, Xenophanes, agreed with me. I met him when he was making his way from Colophon to Elea to escape the Persians. Better than brute strength of men, or horses, he said, is the wisdom that is mine.

For three days I tried to teach them at their sixty-ninth Olympiad, where there was always a good crowd. I urged them to believe that the best man chooses enlightenment in preference to all else, but they chose to glut themselves like cattle…calling me names like the Dark One, the Obnoxious One. You don't have to listen to me, I said. Listen to the Logos. But they remained thrilled by the world of appearances, which is the way of a barbarian soul. And they threw stones at me and expelled me from their Olympiad.

II

Headed west toward Pyrgos, then changed my mind and turned south. Walked until my heels were burning inside my old sandals. Stopped near Krestena as the sun was setting. Didn't enter the village, though. Didn't want to see anyone.

Found a beehive that must have fallen out of a cypress tree. Not sure how long it had been on the stony ground.

Inside the fading dusk light, I smashed it with a rock. There were no bees, so I had my way with it…gorging on the honey and sensing, at the same time, that I was losing the golden thread. Not yet, I said aloud.

Leaned back against the cypress and tried to sleep after the darkness closed in, but felt ill. Told myself to get used to it. Maybe the honey sickness would help me see the hidden harmonies.

Awoke to scratch my shoulder against the tree bark. Dreamed of Hermadorus…how we used to massage each other's backs as we waited for dawn to come, sitting atop the eastern wall of the agora. Imagined we would be like that forever.

Hermadorus…more dear than moonlight, ever since we were boys in Ephesus. But the Ruling Twenty decided he was a threat and banished him from the city, because he excelled at seeing the truth…and smelling their lies. And that is why the voice of the many should never rule, but rather the voice of the one who is wise.

I left, too. Repudiated my family position and riches, letting my younger brother take over, and began my search for Hermadorus, and for the Logos, which sometimes seemed like the same thing.

And after all the years, Hermadorus is still gone from me. And the divine Logos, rarified above the universal fire, has eluded me as well. I only know there is more evil in the world than good. And though they may seem like two sides of the same coin, evil is more profound. And men, with their barbarian souls, have forgotten how much nature loves to hide…with everything flowing and nothing abiding. As I told Hermadorus when we were young, you cannot put your foot in the same river twice. And he—I can't put my foot in the same river once.

I loved him for that, and still do inside this naked vestibule of night where things come to pass beyond seeing, through greater compulsion and greater strife...the universe becoming and becoming until it seems too much to bear...beneath the eternal fire that rekindles and extinguishes itself, and then rekindles...convulsing the universe in pain and then throwing it apart, everything endlessly retiring and advancing, because fire lives in the death of earth and air in the death of fire and water in the death of air and earth in the death of water...but fire still pilots all things. So always again—the glint of sunlight.

Hermadorus and I were once within the holy light above the fire, like a dry beam risen from the dampness and dark to transcend the finite sky. Because even though the way up and the way down are the same, the way up is better...if one believes in an absolute. But I don't anymore. And when the earth melts into the sea, it will be the same amount as when the sea hardens into the earth. And I, Heraclitus....

And if opposition were to cease, all things would dissolve and perish, but the fire would remain eternal. And I, Heraclitus....

And when I am gone, they will endeavor to call me a god, but I will no longer hear their voices, like the mind forgets to recognize the wind, or the day forgets another darkness...sensing the uncertain truth for the last time once more. And I, Heraclitus....

Unless I encounter just one man who hears me, even if he is just a boy. But maybe it would be the same again, sounding like a child's wail behind a desert rock...full-blooded, throbbing in the fiery second. Forgetting just then that the souls in Hades perceive by smelling, which is why corpses are more fit to be thrown out than dung.

III

Woke up with the sun beating heavy on me. Still feeling ill, and thirsty....

Stood slowly and drank some water from the animal skin I stole from the Olympians. The water was warm and rancid. Drank it out of necessity, cursing Thales and his sham belief that water is the first principle in the universe, just because moisture is in all things. Even believing that heat is generated out of moisture.

Would like to talk to ask him about the moisture in my urine, and in this sorry sack I filled from the Alpheus River.

All things moist in some way…but only because fire, the true first principle, allows moisture to come into being before destroying all things back into heat and light. Things seeming to return to water…? The Logos tells us otherwise.

And the fool, Thales, even believing the gods themselves were blended from water.

The truth about the gods? They learned to rule the Earth through fire. And when their time passed, fire itself became a god.

And I, Heraclitus, would like to debate Thales, if he had not already evaporated into fire…the moisture drained from his entrails, his soul blasted into dust.

Urinated against the tree. Walked around the rotting beehive, repulsive in the bright sun, and headed into an olive grove for shade. Was unsure how I would find my way without the road, but aimed in the direction of the Kivouria Mountains to the south.

By mid-day, I was starving and my water sack empty. Was determined to keep walking….

Used to believe I could walk myself into well-being and walk away from every illness. Often walked myself into my best thoughts. And no thought so onerous that I could not walk away from it. While the more one sits still, the more one feels ill.

All that seems hollow to me now. Except for this—if I stop walking, I will die.

Came across a circular patch of herbs growing between two trees. They could be the kind that are very good for a man's health, or the kind that make a man insane. Smelled a bit like thyme, but knew it wasn't. Ate a few handfuls, then lay to rest on top of them, staring up through the trees. Didn't feel thirst anymore.

Closed my eyes. Could feel my green bed moving…left to right…edging me away from where I knew I was.

Stand up, you old patch of a philosopher, I commanded. But couldn't budge a limb.

After a few minutes, though, I stood fine and climbed with alacrity to a barren hilltop. On the other side, a downhill path. *Must lead to a stream.* So I loped down the tilting path…. Could hear my hips creaking with each step. Reached above and grabbed some unripe olives from the branches. Ate the flesh and spit out the pits. Then decided to swallow the pits as well, saying aloud, *Sustenance*….

A stream was there, beneath the shady green. Shallow and moving through dappled sunlight. Filled my water sack and splashed my face. Then decided to lift my cassock and sit in the cool water to make everything down below holy again. Purgation by water, you bastard Thales.

Laid back to rinse my hair. If I turned over, I could drown. And then Thales….

Had trouble sitting up, so rolled sideways onto some rocks, my cassock still above my waist. Didn't have the strength to pull it down. The vengeance of the universe was pressing me into the earth.

Witness the great Heraclitus, a voice said. The river rocks passing through his flesh into his bones. He's philosopher carrion now, waiting for the birds. A rotting husk of a man, smelling into the sky…his liquid self seeping into the dark soil hidden from the fire that could have purged him upward.

Where is the Logos now? I heard myself say without words, because my mouth was swallowing a small round stone tasting of lichen…my voice less than whispers fluttering beneath the shade of the wavering olive leaves. The trees themselves moving away, seen through one eye before the final closing.

Hermadorus stood over me, shaking our bedcovers into the sun to freshen them before hanging them over the archway until evening. He stared at me for a moment before turning toward a pulse of white light. And he was gone.

Accepted the truth for the first time—Logos was a lie. And Heraclitus a fool sinking into the rock-wasted rump of the world.

I *am* the Dark One.

My sacred belief—that I was the first to be guided by the divine light of reason—was just another myth.

Logos did not mean the end of myth. Logos is a myth.

The great truth—with eyes closed and crotch penetrated by moist rocks—everything is in flux. Nothing is absolute.

Should have told the Olympians a story instead....

Once there was a god, neither male nor female, who descended from the fire through the light of reason, destroying all other myths and all other gods, until one day a dark-minded man told the story of this god before rolling his half-naked body into the rocks while his spirit descended into the moist earth, and the memory of the god frittered away under the unripe olives....

Dreamed that I stood up, walked forward, hit my forehead on the glossy bark of a tree and fell...

...and the god's name was....

After that, nothing left to remember.

...We are as beasts, and the universe, a random fire beyond its own control, with nothing above so no one can say the word logos, and he who did died after the river rocks pierced his head, and the water retreated over his body, because of Thales.

...Remember once being the lover of the universe...that climbed on top of me when my cassock was above my waist, hands unable to move and that's how I fathered the false principle of reason, like when the sky climbed on top of Earth and fathered Eros, who planted the urge to become in all things, until the god Logos grew to fear Eros and her fecund becoming, so he took her by force and ascended beyond the sun...and when I looked back at Heraclitus, who was once the wisest of men, he appeared as a naked beast, because he failed to understand how immortals can become mortals and mortals become immortals living in each other's death by the power of fire allowing the first breaths of life over and over again....

...And the above is no longer the light I loved, and the below is a suffering curse of beauty that fades at my touch, while the fire bolt pilots all things cursed and beautiful, without me....

...And the elements never cease to expand and perish. And nothing wears out...making me wonder if I should retreat to the temple of Artemis and play knuckle-bones with the boys while the Ephesians stand around wondering—who is this man who acts like a god?

Why look surprised, you scoundrels? Isn't this a better pastime than taking part in your politics?

...And wherever I was, I thought I shouldn't be. And whenever I left, no one remembered me. Except at Olympia, when they threw stones.

...And I, Heraclitus...self-exilic, living on sickening herbs and lichen and filth-water and dead bees until I have the strength to stop eating and stop drinking and stop moving during the inevitable coming of days...seeing only what I believe without reason, and stopping where no one can deny me....

...Blood lymphing along, a gathering of limbs and organs...cassock back over my knees, and remembering there was once a strong body and the foolish belief I could walk into health....

...Bending over to drink the clear stream, wondering if someone sees me from behind....

...I, Heraclitus, wraith of a man...barely remnants enough to be considered Being...with too much still going on all around...

I decided to follow the stream.

IV

I arose and walked, the wound on my forehead still throbbing.

Glad I had bathed. Felt nearly holy. Needed sustenance but vowed only to drink water and chew on tree bark.

The white light from the western sun, piercing through the overhead leaves, seemed fixed in the sky. The only change—the width of the water narrowing as I headed downstream. *Doesn't make sense, unless Thales is torturing me. Because the water coming from the Kivouria Mountains moves toward the Neda River and on to the Ionian Sea.*

Longed to see the great Neda Falls. Remember the old men in the agora talking about it when I was a boy. The Neda seemed so far away then…across the Aegean.

Instead of ineluctably moving to the sea, perhaps the stream sifts away into desert rocks. Perhaps the linear movement of water itself is another myth. Or perhaps the stream loops around so subtly people can't perceive it. The cunning of nature…changing just enough to deceive.

Things happen, but with such little variation that time barely unwinds. Like when I saw the ancient drawings on the battlement walls outside the town of Chora, on the island of Naxos. The drawings depicted sharp island mountains against stark brilliant seas. But when I touched the emery-rock surface, the wall became concave and I walked forward, which Pythagoras would say is impossible. The wall looped around me and the drawings themselves morphed into images of naked men hacking at each other with swords and scythes…dead horses piled around them. *This is the truth of war, on Naxos, where young Zeus was raised in a cave on Mount Zas, and where Dionysus remains forever vigilant…the eternal protector of the Cycladic realm.*

Gazed upward to discern any changes in the canopy of leaves, and that's when I nearly fell on top of her. A crag-faced woman as old as the large rock upon which she lay. Arms and legs spread to her sides, the back of her head inside a niche of stone that seemed to be there for that sole purpose. She had merged right out of the fuscous-colored rock…her bed and her home. Face darkly tanned, body wrapped in a translucent tunic the same color as the rock, and her aged eyes closed. A colored rag, like a bright flower, perched atop her head. Hands brown and gnarled; feet unsandaled, splayed and enseamed. *She doesn't look like a Hellene. Is she a barbarian?*

Backed away, not sure whether to disturb her. Watched for a while to see if there was movement. But there was nothing. Her eyelids—petrified brown petals.

I shifted to the left and then to the right. Knelt to fill my water skin from the stream and flopped it against her foot. Nothing.

The sun had begun moving again. The hot light breaking through a patch of leaves and beating upon her face.

I withdrew a few paces and considered dancing for her. Maybe she would see me through her stone eyelids. A decadent dance involving flashing knees and crotch, and a few spins.

Could feel the seconds passing, like drops of hot wax on my shoulders. Two crows were fighting in the treetops; one gave up and flew away.

Decided to touch her face. When my hand got close, she spoke, her eyes still closed—

Are you lost? she asked, her voice sounding more male than female.

Her question weakened me, as if I had been stunned by the aura of a god. I collapsed and tried to sit but ended up lying on my side beneath her.

I'm trying to find my way to the Neda River.

My eyes stared into the rock, not at her.

This empties into a grape field, she said.

And the Neda?

You missed it. The stream forks to the right. You will have to go back.

My spirit gave away, knowing I would have to retreat. But what if she wasn't telling the truth?

I've exhausted myself getting this far, I muttered.

She didn't respond.

Why are you here? I asked.

I'm waiting for them to come for me.

Who?

My people.... They know where I am.

Her body moved for the first time, as if she was going to sit up. Then she seemed to change her mind and reclined back into her rock.

Do you need help? I asked.

You shouldn't be here.

I need to rest a bit, then I'll—

Not now, she interrupted, her head raised from her rock.

Maybe she is going to levitate.

The smell of lavender was in the air.

Even sleepers are collaborators in what goes on in the universe, I said, looking at her stone-closed lids.

You sound like a philosopher, she said. A tired one.

Then she added—

Too late now.

I am Heraclitus, I wanted to say, but no words came out of my mouth and an invisible force rolled me onto my stomach. Tried to kneel, but failed. Raised my hand to touch her, to see if she was flesh or stone. The smell of lavender thickened; nothing else in the air. A pulse of wind pressed through the treetops, curled up the water, and jousted at the side of my body, rolling me like parchment, over and over across rocks and stubs of grass, scratching my face and legs, driving me into dried barley stems that cloyed my skin until the dark spirit lost interest and I could breathe between the brown stalks. Closed my eyes to clear the dust. When I opened them, I was next to her rock again, and she was gone.

My cassock was in tatters; my body burning from the lacerations. Wanted to sit inside the water, but the stream was no more than a few inches.

She was right, I decided. I will have to go back. So I picked up my water skin, which was somehow empty, and limped up the stream that was disappearing during the very moments I stared at it. *Need to hurry. Stay ahead of the demons.... They want to drag me into the abyss and have their way with me.*

V

Found the fork in the stream, which was really a bend in a river. The tributary I followed had completely evaporated.

After soaking for a while to cleanse my lacerations, drank more water than my stomach could hold. With wounded fingers, tugged off a piece of bark from a poplar tree. Tried chewing it. When that seemed impossible, I sucked on the bark. The taste was bitter, so I spit out the bark and picked up a hand-sized stone from the riverbed and licked the lichen from the bottom. The act disgusted me. Is this the best you can do? I cried aloud, my voice sounding alien.

Came across a boulder big enough to die upon. Like the demon-goddess, I planned to petrify into oblivion. Stretched my back convexly atop the unnaturally smooth surface, my neck craning downward making me vulnerable to everything around.

Wondered if my people would come for me…in a lavender crush of wind setting my body free so I could be transformed…my spirit ascending into the eternal fire beyond the finite sky.

Except that I had no people.

Felt a fever coming on…. Nothing to be done. Embarrassed about the state of my cassock. What if someone recognizes the great philosopher Heraclitus looking like petrified filth? But if I never open my eyes, I won't have to see them.

In time, the sun has to fade behind the Kivouria Mountains. Dusk will come, and he will see me here.

VI

The boy's voice seemed to come and go. Then it was a steady stream, as if it had always been….

Maybe it was no voice at all, but the sound of the wind through the fir trees. And if there were fir trees, I was at a higher elevation and had been transformed. Yet how is it I was laying atop a mound of dung?

We use the animal waste to build beehives, the boy said. Then we sell the honey. You had some this morning. There is more in the urn.

I don't remember any honey. And I don't remember this cassock I am wearing.

It's my father's. He keeps an extra one in the cart.

I have never eaten honey.

I think it made you feel better, sir.

There has never been a time…when I would have said, I feel better.

But you do now, sir. Because we are at the Neda Falls. You can see the falls from the cart. Just lift your head.

It is impossible to arrive anywhere.

The Neda Falls, sir. Remember?

This isn't the Neda Falls. The Neda Falls are grand…named after the nymph who took care of the infant Zeus. I've seen falls like this. There is nothing divine here.

You weren't well when I found you on that rock, sir…. I had gone to the stream so Lucienne could have some water.

Lucienne?

My horse.

The name doesn't sound Hellenic. You have a barbarian horse?

My father named her. I was going to take you to my father's house, but you kept screaming, Take me to the Neda Falls! You tried to climb out of the cart. And I, Heraclitus, will not lie on dung, you said. But I kept the cart moving. At the Neda Falls, you said you would prove that Thales was right, and your life was a lie…. Lucienne is tired, sir. Here, let me help you out of the cart.

Don't touch my body. It is foul. I can make it on my own.

I have to leave, sir. My father will be worried. But you are here, where you wanted to be.

Yes, if this really is the Neda Falls…. And if Thales's theory is true, his evidence is disappointing.

The boy turned his cart and stopped.

Sir, I hope you find Hermadorus.

How do you know about him?

You talked of him in the cart…maybe you were dreaming.

Yes, it must have been a dream.

The boy touched Lucienne's gray main and they slowly headed down the hill.

Wished it was later into the feverish night, with the sky glowing red… instead of this incessant white light reminding me of what I no longer want to know…dreaming of relief inside the deep blue, without Thales there to chasten me…and I, Heraclitus, would be just a wisp of memory, the last twitch of a fading hand…past the sleep darkness and the forever light-again-too-soon…all the strange smells and colors of the Earth disappearing, all that was once familiar…until I can barely see myself standing atop the Neda cliff…in that bitch of a moment believing I could hear intermittent thunder from across the Ionian Sea…much too far for an ungodlike man to swim…walking would have to do…each step moving into a different river, and I, Heraclitus….

Tossed my wretched sandals over the falls. I wouldn't need them anymore.

My dejection was powerless to carry me farther…. Couldn't suffer another thought by the man Heraclitus. So I let him go—from the slick mossy rock into the thin blue air. Not really jumping as much as stepping beyond the portico of the false divine.

And the cassock, that was not his, floated above his head like a gray shroud as he descended into Neda's finality…crushing scrotum first into Zeus's sacred pond before battered head snapping back against the water's skin…from pristine blue into the compressed earth where there are no limits to disintegration, and all truths become skeletal for a being who has lived too long under the light….

VII

Floating suspended by the nymphaea, reflected into a crystalline sky… the nymphaea created by Neda, nymph of the river who planted the nymphaea in the soil at the bottom of the pond below the Neda Falls… the river itself miracled into being by Rhea because all of Arcadia was without water.... Uncannily, she touched the ground with the top of a tall cypress tree and a river burst forth...and she named the river after the nymph most dear to her, Neda, who would keep watch over the sacred waters forever flowing over the falls....

Such was the story his mother told him when he was a boy learning to swim in the Pyramu River near Ephesus....

...And how Rhea gave birth to Zeus at the top of Mount Lykaion and hid him from Kronos inside a fennel stalk while she descended to the river where she entrusted her son to Neda, nymph of the indelibly blue waters, who created the nymphaea for the infant-god to sleep softly upon....

...And the Neda nymphaea, through her divine power, never turned dormant in winter—sinking below the surface inside opalescent globules, but flowered throughout the seasons so the Zeus-child could become the greatest of all divine beings....

Eventually, the nymphaea spread across the known world...the barbarians calling them water lilies. But none of them having the power to flower at night through all seasons, only the Neda nymphaea, perfect beyond the gnomonic fantasies of Pythagoras, with their bright pink petals longer than all others, and the inside yellow sepals expressing the geometric quintessence of the divine....

...Like Zeus, he sleeps upon the nymphaea during the slow seconds of the long arching afternoon.... Below him, the nymphaea fruit, which no one sees except the nymph, sink downward after the flower closes at the end of day....

...I, Heraclitus, he thinks, may have failed as a man and philosopher, but not as a god, since my head rests where his once did... He, who mastered the shaft of cypress used by his mother to strike the brown earth into gushing water and later transformed the cypress into his eternal bolt of fire, lives through me.... Because water is the Arche of existence, which I should have learned as a boy, instead of spinning my myth of fire....

...And I, Heraclitus, did not die exposed to the sunlight, head resting on metamorphic rock by the river....

After nothing, I became something again.

VIII

The voice of the boy returned.

Impossible. Nymphaea is for the gods.

I have you, sir.

I am not yet reborn!

You lost my father's cassock.

Still in the same body.

You will have to put your old one on, even though it is falling apart.

Nothing falls apart…out of discord comes harmony, by disease health is pleasant, by evil good is….

I can't understand you, sir. You are mumbling…. You will have to wear it. This isn't Olympia; you cannot ride naked in my cart.

I am walking to the sea…. Go to your father's. Just a moment ago I was nearly divine. But you took me away from the nymphaea.

You were drowning, sir.

I was becoming a god.

You are a man who cannot walk barefoot. Sit in my cart. Lucienne has missed you.

Lucienne?

The boy turned the horse to face me. I would have to step into the river to get around her.

Put this on, sir. Your old cassock.

Every moment a different river, *because opposition keeps all things in motion and brings concord…by hunger satiety, by weariness rest…*and I….

You are mumbling again, sir.

I spoke nothing.

You must teach me.

Do I look like a wise man?

Stepped into the river because the horse would not move. The brown water swirled around my swollen ankles. One step more and I would drop into the depths….

Teach me, and I will take you to the sea.

Why won't you let me die? Then I can—

If you want to walk into the river and drown, sir. I won't stop you this time.... But who should I inform about Heraclitus after his death? Is there anyone?

How do you know my name?

This morning in the back of the cart you kept proclaiming, And I, Heraclitus...

It is hard to fight desire, which gets what it wants at the cost of the soul.

That's it, sir. Teach me. And Lucienne and I will carry you to the sea.

Leave me be, boy.

Standing in the Neda, no longer hearing the great falls. The water, mixing with the filth of the earth, no longer divine. As the sun drops behind low clouds, could feel the chill of dusk coming on, and time itself working against me...with nothing to be done inside the moments of suspension.

The horse moved its head against my bare chest. Lucienne... yes, I remember.

I will go with the horse.

Sat on the seat of the cart. Shivering. The boy threw my old cassock around my shoulders.

Follow the river until it ends, I commanded.

The boy nodded and Lucienne began to move. Things beside us passed slowly as the curtains of dusk closed around. Things in front didn't change at all but just faded. And the river, flowing strongly, gradually disappeared into the gloom.

The graying power subsumes all. If there was a god for it, I would be her servant.

What about your father?

I'm sure he is wondering why I am not home. But he always tells me, Helagon, you must learn to make your own decisions.

Helagon? That is your name?

And I, Helagon, will build the beehives after I take you to the sea.

You're taking me to Elea, but your home is in...?

Rodina.

Heraclitus has nothing to give you, Helagon.

That is why you will teach me as we make our way.

You want to learn from a man who threw himself over the Neda Falls?

You did that because you have too much wisdom. Now you can unburden yourself.

The Neda Falls was not so great. A vibrant rush of air through the body, then blackness…until you drew me back into the world of mortals.

You didn't go over the great falls, sir. You went over the secondary run-off…half the height of the great falls. I took you there because I knew you were going to jump, and I wanted you to live.

But the nymphaea?

They are in the ponds beneath both falls.

There is no way to die without flesh, and nothing exists more than anything else, so nothing is more real than Lucienne….

What did you say, sir?

Her haunches move with a patient rhythm, in syncopation with the well-tuned universe. The truth is with Lucienne, not in the nymphaea…. And she is beyond our oldest idea of the gods…this flea-bitten gray horse, no longer even gray, but aged-white, is herself a god, because gray cannot subsume her….

I'm not quite hearing you, sir.

You want to learn about the Logos, boy? Of the slow plodding into eternity, shoulders in opposition to the shifting rhythm of the head, the withers waving at time, rear hooves dragging in the dust because there is no point in expending any more effort. And the same primal dust gathering into the feathers of the front fetlocks that no one ever sees….

Sir, are you talking of Lucienne or the Logos?

We live beneath the divine Logos and the realm of eternal fire… things grow and devour, change and die and become again…and after Helagon saved me from the fire and the water, the truths of Heraclitus and Thales appeared as one. But they truly are not. And the nymphaea, which I love more than the nectar of Aphrodite, seduced an old man's graying mind….

No one knows the depths of the soul, which escapes as vapor from the moist earth, and that is why a dry soul is the wisest and the best.

The purest—a fine beam of light. So it is death for souls to become water, which is why Thales is a lie....

And I, Heraclitus, will teach the boy to see the hidden harmony that is more obscure, but superior, to what is obvious, and that is why people do not see that opposition creates agreement within the self, as the great harmony bends back the lyre of time....

I'm only hearing fragments of your voice, sir.

That is enough.

Perhaps we should stop. It is too dark for Lucienne to see, and she mustn't injure a leg.

Even gods need to rest.

We'll sleep atop the mound in the cart. I have rags to cover us, and I have more honey.

I could live on honey...and the bark from ancient trees.

We will make it to the Ionian Sea tomorrow.

That will be enough.

And you will teach me more tomorrow?

Yes, following Lucienne.

IX

Sat in the cart with the boy watching the Neda River funnel into the sea. No one in sight, just wide stretches of raw sand.

Where are the mortals? And the boy—

The village of Elea is near. I'm going there to trade honey for bread.

I won't be seeing you again. I'm walking north on the beach until I meet my old friend, Hermadorus. And he and I will—

You can't go anywhere barefoot, sir. And you are weak.

I don't need sandals. I'll be walking on sand.

Wait for me. I'll be back with food and fresh water.

For the second time, the boy known as Helagon departed from me.

Didn't walk far before my body refused my commands. Had to lie down on the infinite granules in the midday heat. *Why fight it. Just hand the flesh over. Here, underneath the myriadic universe, waiting for the fire to consume....*

What happened at Olympia, that is the question. With too many implications I cannot grasp, my mental powers escaping me....

In the morning, saying the same truths as the day before. So they threw rocks at me; cursed a man for not being humble. Heraclitus, the Dark One...because I only see by the light of the Logos, which left me bereft after I tasted rocks and the poison of exile...the eternal fire never really inside me and divine reason a madman's rumination... and I am he and I am not he, Heraclitus of Ephesus...lying on the sand-step of a tilting universe, tethered between the dome of fire and the roiling sea....

If called before them, I would confess, I have heard many stories of the sky and Earth, but nothing like the one pristine word—logos. So I invented nothing.

Learned to talk to the Earth and sky, to join forces with them after seeing too much abiding and receding...and when I am gone, they will remember just enough to know what they have forgotten, with the truth of their exhausted world frittering away in thin smoke before their half-closed eyes, and I, for the millionth time licking my dry lips, dreaming, that in a moment, it will all go away....

The boy returned. He stands above me, sun glaring beyond his head.

The old man has not traveled far from the river, he thinks.

In one hand he holds an urn of water, in the other—

I have white Athenian flat bread. Winner of the laurel, the best there is.

I have heard, but never eaten....

Brushed the sand from my hands and received the bread. It had been a long time. My stomach flinched in revulsion. But I mastered myself and swallowed again.

Raised my head and stood up next to the boy who no longer had his cart. Standing behind Lucienne was another beast, black as Cerberus. I had seen its kind before.

What have you done?

I traded the cart and the honey for bread and a mule. Father will be happy since he believes Lucienne's useful days are over.

Lucienne cannot be measured.

That's why she's yours.

No one can own Lucienne!

She will be your companion while I return to my father's house. You can ride on her back.

Moved to touch Lucienne's gray-white mane, glancing at the beast behind her.

There were mules at Olympia. They competed in harness races for the first time. Most folks hadn't seen one before. But I had, back in—

I wanted a donkey. But the man only had mules. He said they have been breeding them in Ionia…near Ephesus.

Homer was telling the truth when he spoke of mules in his Iliad.

Turned away from Cerberus and put both of my arms around the neck of Lucienne.

Help me.

Helagon lifted me onto Lucienne. Too painful to sit upright, so I laid forward with my head to the side of her neck. Could smell the rank mustiness of her. Breathed Lucienne in….

The boy slung a water pouch over my back and tied some of the bread to the strap. Lucienne moved away on her own, her haunches slowly wrenching back and forth. Behind, the boy's voice for the last time—

I will be back in a few days with a new cart and will find you.

Should have thanked him, but he knew I did without saying.

Sank into the weight of Lucienne so that the weight of Heraclitus hardly existed, and she moved incrementally northward up the beach…my eyes staring through the blinding sunlight across the dark cerulean sea.

After an interminable time, came to a creek where Lucienne could drink. Slept there for the night, stretched out on the sand, my head propped on Lucienne's balding stomach, which sank inward and then lifted outward, with her slow breathing.

At dawn, Lucienne and I finished the bread and water. There was nothing left.

Helagon would not be arriving with reinforcements.

Fell back asleep until we were startled by a group of young children bathing naked in the sea. Two women dressed in stiff white tunics watched over them. These were the first humans we had seen. But they were not aware of us. Perhaps Lucienne and I were outside their dimension.

Crawled onto Lucienne's back. She arose slowly and willfully. After advancing a few steps, the children clapped at her achievement. Come back, sir. We want to pet your old horse, they shouted. We were not invisible; children just don't see strangers until they are already past them.

By afternoon, Lucienne was moving up the beach at a quicker pace, as if she knew I was anxious to see Hermadorus.... *And he will be waiting under his tent, a table spread with figs and olives and salted fish....*

Arrived at Katakolo Beach just before sunset. Knew it was Katakolo because of the turn into a peninsula. Lucienne ambled directly into the west, Helios glaring into us like his yellow light was setting for the last time. Lucienne slowed into near stillness, tired beyond the end of her years.

A flint away from nihilo.

Drifted across the sand, the wind wafting at my back, half blinded by the expanding orb on the orange horizon. Bits of my cassock frayed away. Anticipated being naked by the time we reached the water.

In the old days, would have believed Poseidon was drawing the great gray horse back into the curl of the waves, where it all began....

Imagined my old beliefs spooling out of me, plowing a furrow of sand toward the unfurrowed sea. The sun, spiraling beyond, somehow increasing its heat in order to make me regret all that

I had doubted. I…Heraclitus…*a dwindling sum by negation, with weakening thoughts arriving too late, so I could never be the sun's death-lover, because I had been seduced by the nymphaea…lost my focus on the Arché of Eternal Fire, which I should have affirmed from the bowels up…. Fire, the absolute that sears away all deities….*

…And that is why the sun remains fixed above the horizon, for a man whose wisdom was gleaned by no one, so Heraclitus can feel eternity. Heraclitus, who understood the terrible process of becoming inside an infinite realm of possibility…the tedious making and unmaking of moments, marrow splitting into blood rivers, sinews fired into flesh… with fire itself not the miracle, but allowing all other miracles to exist… the wonderfully combustive aphasias of truth…seeing without seeing, from the days when Heraclitus could feel himself inside the frenzy with Hermadorus, the terrible becoming right then, in a way the poets never understood….

…Opened my eyes for the millionth time to witness the orange-brown sky flaking into ashes, while Lucienne's neck sways in rhythm with the long sequacious waves….

…There are no more questions for Heraclitus, who mutters in a trance—fetlock furrow feather, fetlock furrow feather…while the pebbles of sand cast needle-like shadows, just before the sun ineluctably passes through the last stream of clouds….

…So much owed to the boy….

…Just one desire left—to drift past the carcass of a departed god. But the throng of memories gets in the way….

…Holding my breath, thinking with blood until I can see through the black glass the Egyptians gave me, sweeping away the derelict dust of ages until…the will to begin again….

X

Ahead, a man sits on a bench close to the breaking waves. From a distance, it could be him.

When he turns toward me, I can see he is barbarian. Black screw-tape hair, dark skin, wide forehead.

Lie down on the bench old man, he says calmly, and rest. I will stand for a while.

I obey. Lucienne lies down, too, tumbling over like a dog too tired to care.

Have some water. Here, in the urn.

Not for me. For the horse.

He carefully pours water into a clay bowl for Lucienne who sits up to drink and then lies back down and lolls her head to the side.

What are you waiting for? I ask.

The sun finally released itself and began dropping into the Earth. I closed my eyes.

My friend to return from the island.

A fisherman?

Yes.

What's the name of the island?

Zakynthos. If you turn your head, you will see it.

Half-opened my eyes.

The sunset is blinding.

Look again, old man. There's a volcano on the island sacred to Zeus.

Yes. I see it. How far away is the island?

Half a day's sail.... I see my friend now, tacking in our direction against the stiff wind. With luck, he will make it to shore while there is still light.

I sat up. A strip of cassock fell away from my shoulder.

Have you ever heard of a man named Hermadorus?

An older man, like you?

I nodded.

He had a school here on the Katakolo Peninsula. But the Lacedaemonians, who claim this part of the Peloponnesus for their own, burned it down because they believed he was sheltering rebels from Pylos.

And Hermadorus?

He escaped to Zakynthos Island.

He's still there?

Unless he is dead.

Could your friend take me there in his boat?

You will have to ask him.

What is his name?

Agoria.

He is Hellenic or barbarian?

Barbarian.

Good. Except for the boy, I have given up on the Hellenes. Tomorrow, then, as soon as the sun is up.

You will need to pay him.

He will take my horse, Lucienne, as well.

I don't think he will agree to that.

Lucienne will lie down inside his boat and not move.

For hours?

She is good at that.

The man looked at Lucienne whose head had fallen to the side in sleep.

She's an unusual horse.

She is a god.

Perhaps he will take her. But you will have to pay him.

Of course.

But I can see you have nothing.

On the way to Zakynthos, I will teach Agoria. That will be my payment.

Teach him what?

Of the Logos.

Who are you?

I am the philosopher Heraclitus, of Ephesus.

Chapter Nine
PONT-AUTHOU

I

McCuade is with me when I feel him fading away, and absent when he and I are one.

II

At The Lion's Head in Galway, waiting to catch the bartender's eye—a thin, unfinished-looking man, blond-streaked hair falling diagonal across his forehead.

Three young women at the other end of the bar are talking to him, not in his interest to look my way. Can hear their voices, dissonant, cacophonous…. They are unsure where they want to be. And he is nodding yes and yes.

Each woman desires him in her own way and that is why they aren't going anywhere.

He finally delivers my pint, his eyes letting me know he is willing to chat. But I look past him, through the mirror, at a plump couple standing next to the sashed window. The man has his hand inside her back pocket and tugs her toward his crotch. He wants her right there. But she is indifferent, and gazes toward two old Irishmen with their fiddles by the front door. They are singing a ballad about the young lass Kate from Connemara, lost in the fog upon the moor of Loughanure.

Remember driving across Loughanure on my way to Malin Head. He was inside my mind, and I had to ask questions, follow signs, quest for him.... So much palaver and lies. Crucial to know the difference. And easy to miss him after he is already gone. *Aye, that's it exactly*, I can hear him say. And *Nitimur in vetitum*, the splendid is that which is forbidden.

One of the girls stares at me. Haven't obliged her by looking back. She is not moonfaced. *Strawberries, she says, he gave me....*

Wanting to believe it was I, not he, who gave.... But not I is what I hear.

In the cool of early morning, tired-looking men will arrive from their camps to do everything that needs to be done under the sun....

She has taken my hand and leads onward...past rows of lustrous grapes, not made of flesh...rows symmetrical and infinite. She desires to choose just one row among them all. And the years seem to revolve backward as we pass each vine row....

Much closer to the manoir house than I remember. Can see the balcony railings outside the windows. Remember the day I threw my old boots out the upstairs window into the freshly plowed field. Did not want to wear them anymore.

In the morning, the boots were gone. And in the evening, on a narrow street in the village, saw an old Frenchman wearing them as if they had always been his. He seemed more like me than I can remember....

Beneath the shocking cerulean sky, she drops me to my knees. This row's perfect, she says, her eyes luminous. She lays me back gently as if I were a young boy being settled in for a nap. Next to me, a dim cluster of grapes seems to sway as if we are on a skiff, naked among the swells. Her moon face rises above...blocks the sun. And in her motion, forward and back, she loses balance, because the Earth itself is rising and falling.

She reaches upward to grab at the fine green netting someone has dropped from above to keep the birds away from the ripening fruit. Her eyes close, her head lolls backward...her pale body undulates in rhythm with the Earth.

At the end of her journey, she makes no sound, but drags the netting down upon us. The canopy ensconces completely; we have become a world.

Her body still...the Earth and sky still. Cosmopsis is in effect. When it ends, the moments will march forward once more through the arc of time, and dozens of wild doves will fly from inside the melting green net, upward...a widening funnel into the illimitable blue....

III

On vacation?

No.

Traveling then?

Aye.

From Scotland?

Was up in Malin Head.

I'm from Malin Head. Doagh Island.

Doagh Island?

Two miles south of Malin.

You ever hear of a man named McCuade?

There was a McCuade family from Doagh. Maggie and Joseph.... She was from Malin Head; he was from Scotland.

Did they have a son?

Aye.... Is in his forties now.

Do you remember his name?

His parents died a long time ago.

Could it be Cal?

Maybe.... I should know, he was here last night.

At The Lion's Head? You talked with McCuade and don't know his first name?

Don't need names. We are both from the same wee bits of Malin. Said he was on his way to Normandy...taking the ferry from Portsmouth.

IV

Never should have ceased my pursuit of him...but my return flight got in the way.

Could feel His presence drifting from me.... Suddenly, then, He is there.

Never should have stopped believing in the Garage Wall Man....

And he will be waiting for me, limned by the streetlight, lying against the wall like he is posing for Manet...to tell me, after all of this, why he lied.

But I already know. And then it will be as if he never was....

V

Took the ferry from Rosslare to Pembroke, and then another from Portsmouth to Le Havre, because that was the way Gareth, the Galway bartender, said McCuade would go. And I didn't doubt him, even though I wanted to.... Perhaps Gareth's itinerary was a McCuade vision translated into geographic truth.

But once I left Le Havre, there were no visionary directions to follow, and I had no idea where in Normandy to go.

Opened the map and balanced it against the dashboard. The absurdity of the arbitrary set in.... Remembering, this is how it begins—whimsy contaminated by desire until one forgets how easy it is for nothingness to parade around as something....

Attempted to refold the map. Gave up and threw it on the passenger seat.

Drove until I reached Honfleur, where I would have to decide whether to turn east toward Rouen or west toward Caen.

Parked on Rue de la Bavole. Could sense the ribbons of time raveling around me before frittering away in disappearing silver strands....

An old man in a brown hat and too-large coat limped slowly up the street. He hardly seemed to be progressing. A few old women in white babushkas sat on a doorstep, their faces grim and unflinching. *Something has changed.*

Shadows from the late sun were pasted on the left side of the cobbled street, which wasn't cobbled before, and two stuffed white clouds remained stationary overhead.

I couldn't read the names above the storefronts even though I knew the language. The letters seemed to blur into black lines against a disintegrating gray. Except for a sign directly to my right—DENREES. I knew that word…an old-style French store that sold basic commodities. But when I stepped closer to look inside the window, nothing was there.

You'll get to know the words, she said, but not the accent…. Inside my sixth-floor garret at the Hotel de l'Avenir on Rue de Gay Lussac, pres Le Jardin du Luxembourg, Paris. Il y a quarante ans….

Ca va bien.

She touched my cheek as I stared through the small, angled window in my cramped room…. Could see the endless slate clouds fixed above the Pantheon. When I turned back, she was lying upon the bed, curled on her side, facing the wall, wearing nothing but her boots…her auburn pixie hair falling slightly across her chin that appeared chaulkish in the fading light. Funny, an English girl wearing cowboy boots…sometimes leaving them on when I was inside her on the narrow bed beneath the feeble gray light coming through the window, the glass striated with grime.

I am in Honfleur, because….

Honfleur…so many famous painters drawn here by the buildings and quays inside the mystically colored late afternoon sunlight.

I remembered Monet's darkly sculptural painting, *Rue de la Bavole*, without ever seeing it. Because McCuade loves that painting….

He is performing a second miracle for me. I am inside Monet's *Rue de la Bavole*.

And even though he refuses to acknowledge me, McCuade is allowing me to remember something he has loved. While he, no doubt, is drawing upon my memories.

From time to time, Monsieur McCuade lives in Honfleur, on Rue de la Bavole. Parks his Citroen in front of no. 22. At one point, he obsesses too much about the Monet painting. His friends complain.... No, McCuade has no friends, just people that somehow see him.

McCuade...not only a poet and philosopher, but a painter. Et il habite la maison vingt et deux, ou il peint la porte vert. And I will find his green door. All I have to do is walk along Rue de la Bavole like a flaneur....

Locked the rental car and headed up the slight hill, past the doddering old man in the brown hat who could tip over at any moment.

The shadows rapidly expanded beyond the narrow street; the sky turned pastel green. Could feel myself slipping away...canceling out what I was before...moving into a perilous realm where being itself is difficult to ascertain....

VI

An old washerwoman opens the green door before I can knock twice. She has orange hair piled beneath her babushka, and a creased sun-weathered face.

Monsieur McCuade. Il vit ici?

Mais, non McCuade...peut etre, vous voulez dire Monsieur Maquadrian?

Maquadrian? Et il est a peintre?

Mais Oui!

And his room nombre?

Nombre trois, mais vous n'allez pas la maintenant. Il n'est pas la...j'est ecoute lui dernier...le sien bruyant trace de pas sur le escaliers...mais, le matin, il était parti.

I'd still like to see his chambre.

His name is Claude Maquadrian...he works at a studio on Rue de la Bavole, house no. 22. A thirty-year-old Spanish seamstress is often his model, probably his mistress, too.... Don't remember his paintings of her, but her name is Soncia.

Pushed past the old woman, toward the steep wooden stairs that seemed familiar. Could hear her yelling behind me, Arrêtez! Arrêtez!

At the first step, I changed my direction and veered toward the storage area behind the stairs.

I know where I am going....

In the half shadow, beneath the angled ceiling, an easel with a painting I recognized—Boudin's *Seaside, Port of Honfleur*, 1860.

I desired to touch it—

Ne vous touchez pas, monsieur. S'il vous plaît, ne pas toucher!

The painting was still moist.

C'est impossible! I proclaimed, like I was a Frenchman.

You must leave, monsieur. Maintenant!

That is a Boudin, I said in a doctrinaire way. How? Comment se peut-il? McCuade did not paint this.

Non, c'est Monsieur Maquadrian. Il l'a peint...plusieurs fois. Cent fois il l'a peint...pour prouver que c'est sa peinture, pas celle de Boudin.... C'était un mensonge, monsieur. Boudin était un mensonge. Pendant tant d'années....

So, McCuade has been a painter for a century and a half, that's what you are saying? And everyone knew him as Boudin. All of Honfleur.... And now he lives here and keeps painting the same painting. There is even a museum named after McCuade—Le Musée Eugène Boudin. I can go there, you know.

The old woman slapped me across the legs with a broom, as if that was an acceptable way to get someone to leave.

Je pars pour l'instant, madame. Je pars pour l'instant. But I will wait outside for Monsieur Maquadrian, for Monsieur Boudin, for Monsieur McCuade.

Mais on ne sait jamais quand il reviendra. Jamais connu....

No one knows when he will return? I can still wait in my car, just to see. Juste pour voir....

But once in my car, I knew I wouldn't wait for him. And I wouldn't visit his museum, either.

I stared at the useless map on the other seat, and that's when the aporia set in...with no clear way ahead.

VII

The gendarme rapped his knuckles on my window. He would not stop until I opened my eyes and looked at him.

You cannot sleep ici…in your car, monsieur.

All right, all right, I mouthed and waved him off. He crossed the street and stood statue-like, watching me.

Picked up the map and pretended to stare at it. It was nearly twilight and hard to see. So I put the map down and closed my eyes again. Within moments the gendarme was back.

What are you doing, monsieur? he asked with his heavy French accent and sad mouth, like I had hurt his feelings by closing my eyes a second time.

I rolled the window down half-way.

I am waiting for Monsieur McCuade to return to his house. Nombre twenty-two. It is important I meet with him.

Ah, monsieur…. We, too, have been watching for him…. Un long moment. Mais, we always seem to miss him.

You mean the painter in number twenty-two?

Exactment. He has many…troubles. We need to talk to him. Evidently, he comes and goes.

In the dusk-light, the gendarme seemed to change. His shape darkened and I noticed his old-style sideburns for the first time.

You have a problem with him, monsieur?

Oui. He has taken over…things that were mine. Il a repris tout.

I am not surprised, monsieur. Still, you cannot sleep in your car, not on Rue de la Bavole! I give you a number. Téléphone in a few days and we can tell you if we have seen him. Ca va?

He pulled out a stub of pencil and on a stained piece of paper wrote down a number, sixteen digits. I placed it next to the map on the passenger seat.

Bonsoir, monsieur. Bonsoir.

The gendarme retreated across the street and resumed his statue-like stance, leaning slightly against a gray lamppost.

I pretended to look at the map again. Considered closing my eyes to see how many times we could repeat the charade until it became completely dark and he would no longer be able to see my face.

Started the car engine without my own volition. Was thinking about one thing, trying to remember just one thing…decades ago, after a year in Paris, spending a week at an old manoir in Normandy being restored by my friend, Jim. He was a Vietnam War veteran who had been studying at the Sorbonne on the G.I. Bill. The manoir was in a small village sixty miles west of Paris. I took two trains to get there…to get to Pont-Authou. At the time, I never thought, I am going to Normandy. But rather, I am going to Pont-Authou.

Is a week too long? I asked.

And Jim—stay as long as you like. There are many rooms at the manoir.

Years later, I remembered my week at the manoir as the stuff of personal folklore…a story to be told when the occasion seemed right. And told less often…until Pont-Authou was nearly forgotten.

McCuade remembered for me, while I waited outside nombre vingt-deux, Rue de la Bavole…McCuade believed everything was différent après Pont-Authou. Or perhaps I believed, sui generis, without him.

Turned on the interior light to study the map in earnest. Even put on my glasses to verify more meticulously. Pont-Authou—at the center of Normandy. And that's where I had to go because that's where McCuade already was. McCuade…remembering myself just before me.

Monsieur Claude Maquadrian left his chambre à 22 Rue de la Bavole before dawn, the old washerwoman hearing his footsteps down the stairs, but not seeing him because she never sees him, and the gendarme not seeing him either. And McCuade left another Seaside, Port of Honfleur *behind.*

Gareth was right—McCuade was in Normandy. McCuade was at the manoir. And I am remembering him in Honfleur as he is remembering me in Pont-Authou. The significance of Pont-Authou to be revealed by McCuade as he unfolds my past for me. McCuade, one step ahead of who I am. McCuade, for the first time, pursuing me more intensely than I was pursuing him…until the point where he and I arrive as one.

Couldn't catch my breath after dying for a moment in Honfleur…. But managed to release my foot from the brake… and the car slowly idled along Rue de la Bavole. Rolled down my window to hail the gendarme.

Bonsoir, mon ami! I am going to Pont-Authou. Monsieur McCuade is waiting for me there. Nous allons enfin nous rencontrer. I will tell McCuade you have been watching for him. Mes salutations, mon gendarme!

He didn't move his head, and it was too dark to see his face. Perhaps he didn't hear me. So he would never know how I fulfill McCuade, who cannot be enclosed…and McCuade endures because He abides within.

Do you understand that, my dear gendarme? Comprenez-vous?

VIII

Drove south on Route 130. Too dark to tell where Pont-Authou began or if I had missed it.

Instinct told me I hadn't yet arrived. Or maybe I turned without knowing, because a road sign flashed—Route 124.

I am definitely heading east.

Passed another sign—Thierville. A village that was just some large houses set back from the road, all of them darkened.

The aporia of Honfleur had vanished; my being no longer slipping into His. Could sense I was nearing the point where everything begins. *Tranquility of the soul thick upon me…. Yet how false this dimension is. Making me wonder why so many desire to be inside it.*

And the manoir will feel like home again, for a little while…. His real home being across the Irish Sea.

Too soon for that….

The soul never tires of hoarding so much for itself, He said. Or I heard myself asking Him to say. He, always reposed on the other side, across the darkening blue. Reminding me for the millionth time, that one must nearly cease to exist in order to experience His being there. And why we fail at imagining the nonexistence in-between….

Turned south onto Route 92, thinking that would bring me back toward Pont-Authou. Ahead, an orange-yellow hoar light suspended in the fog. Just below the fog, a sign—La Maison Rouge.

I hadn't eaten since morning. McCuade and the manoir could wait.

IX

Bonsoir, monsieur!

Bonsoir.

Vous êtes seul?

Oui. I am alone.

It is late, monsieur. We close soon. Mais, the chef will still cook for you, right over the hearth. But you must choose quickly, so he will not be angry.

Menu, s'il vu plait?

À La Maison Rouge, monsieur, we take care of everything. En pris. Vite, into the courtyard. Tu dois choisir un oiseau…. You must choose a bird.

Too dark to see, but could smell the guano.

Stood still until my eyes adjusted. Dozens of them settling inside the shadows, some into cages, others flocking into the corners of the courtyard. It was hopeless to choose, so I turned back.

He was behind me—

We have many chickens, monsieur. And ducks, grouse, geese, pheasant, quail, pigeons, turkeys…. Shall I choose for you?

Yes.

D'accord. Two grouse, then. One for you and one for your friend.

My friend?

Of course, monsieur. C'est vrai?

Ca va bien. For me and my friend.

A little table was set up just beyond the reception area, as if my friend and I were being placed on display. Before me was a raging open-hearth fire.

I settled into the wooden chair. He appeared again.

Two Scottish red grouse, monsieur. Tu approuves?

He held the grouse upright in his arms, like a man might hold twin babies, his fingers half disappearing into the spectral red and black feathers. The birds were asleep, like babies might have been. Except their heads drooped grotesquely.

What is your name?

Simon.

Simon…those are beautiful birds. Mais, what has happened to them?

They felt nothing, monsieur. Croyez-moi. Et…they are for you and your friend. No?

Yes. For me and Jim.

Jim sat across from me…smiling with lips closed. *He knows what is going on.* Jim is a rock…with his large-featured face and thick black hair.

Simon returned.

The grouse are being prepared, monsieur. In a few minutes they will be roasting before your eyes.

He wanted a positive response from me. But I said nothing. I didn't want to give him that much. And I was anxious to hear what Jim might have to say. Sometimes one has to wait a while before Jim speaks.

Simon continued.

Alors…. En attendant, puis-je vous apporter une carafe de Beaujolais? Oui?

Oui. Parfait.

As soon as he walked away, Jim leaned back in full extension, gesturing with his thick hands.

This place is the greatest! he proclaimed for everyone to hear. But there was only him and me.

You have to love the French, he continued animatedly, leaning in toward me, his eyes squinting with excitement. Nowhere else in Europe would you find this. Only at La Maison Rouge. They kill, dress, and roast the birds right in front of you. And we…we have to help them with the cooking! How beautiful is that?

He broke into a coy smile.

What do you mean, help them? I asked.

Jim rubbed his hands, pushed up on his glasses, and reached for his water.

A ceramic carafe of Beaujolais arrived. This time Simon said nothing. He seemed haughty.

A waiter approached with two wine glasses. He was thin, miserable-looking; his apron streaked with brown stains. Perhaps he was Russian. A few minutes later, he returned with the grouse tightly wrapped in a gray cloth.

I think I've hurt the maître d's feelings, I said quietly to Jim.

Don't worry about him, he bellowed. It's better if he is rude to us. It is the French way. He is being true to himself, and then we must tip him more.

What do you mean?

France is the opposite of America. The French are supposed to be rude. The nastier they are, the more I tip. If they are nice, I give them nothing.

The servant acted as if he didn't hear Jim and stoked the fire violently until the flames raged.

My forehead was sweating, I stood to move our table back. Simon stopped me.

No, monsieur. You must stay close…to tend to the birds. Je suis désolé. The chef has gone home.

I told you we would do the damn cooking, Jim said wryly. They always find a way—the chef has gone home, the chef is très busy. I don't believe there really is a chef at La Maison Rouge.

Then why do you come here?

La Maison Rouge is in another dimension, Jim said, as if he were searching for religious affirmation.

The servant bent over to unwrap the birds. His back was to us, so I couldn't see what he was doing. A few minutes later, he limped away and there were our beautiful grouse—inside the fire on the spit, the fat already dripping.

I didn't remember seeing the skewer spit before. I turned to ask Jim, but he was gone, perhaps to the salle de bains. When I gazed back at the fire, there was only a single grouse on the spit.

The waiter returned carrying a metal pot, a brush, and an oven mitt.

Vous devez arroser toutes les cinq minutes et faire une rotation toutes les cinq minutes. Ou tout sera ruiné.

I barely understood his command. Something about basting and rotating. And if the grouse were ruined, it would be my fault. He left the pot at my feet. It was filled with gray cloying butter and French herbs. There was an effluvium of pine. Perhaps rosemary….

I sipped the wine, which was flat and thin. I liked it. There was no napkin, so I wiped my mouth on the tablecloth since no one was around.

Reached into the fire and brushed the grouse with the sauce. Then put on the oven mitt and rotated the spit until the two grouse were on their backs.

When I sat back in my chair, Jim was there, but he looked different. He could have been anyone….

Sometimes I eat here alone, he said dreamily. I snap the neck of the bird myself, out in the courtyard. The kitchen staff come to watch. They love me for it. When we come back again, you will do that, and they will love you, too.

No, I never would….

You will. And you will feel, for a moment, like a god.

He paused and turned sideways to baste the grouse and rotate the spit slowly without the glove. *He knows what he is doing. And he is definitely not Jim.*

Fais attention! You will burn your hand.

I don't feel it, he said. Je suis magnifique. I'm wondering, though, which one is yours and which one mine?

A bowl of sliced French bread appeared on the table and a small ramekin of butter smoothed perfectly across the top. Using his thin index finger as a knife, he dipped in and spread the butter onto a slice of the baguette.

Simon arrived with a plate of smoked trout piled upon spears of endive.

Your first course, monsieur, he said, his voice passionless.

He walked away. *The maître d' is not the same as before. All because....*

You will love this, the man-who-was-not-Jim said.

He dumped the pink trout from a spear of endive onto another round slice of bread and swallowed in one bite. As he chewed, I stared sideways at him, trying to figure out the man...thin, slightly stooped with a narrow bird-like face and prominent nose, deeply set sharp blue eyes and his gray hair spiked back above his head.

I remembered, when I was younger, how I used to see Jim as a figure forged together over centuries. This man was not the product of centuries but of millennia.... If someone were to see him, would they notice? But one does *see* him...marginally corporeal, an eater of raw fish and, undoubtedly, a delighter in raw flesh, which he swallows with aplomb on a wedge of bread.

From my widening periphery, I believed I could peer through him...across a vertical plane of bluish-gray, the ancient color of infinity.

Which one is yours and which one mine? he calmly asked again, not taking his eyes from the fire.

I looked at the birds.

The one wearing a hat, I said, with a tinge of laughter.

Neither bird is wearing a hat, monsieur, the maître d' remonstrated.

He had been hovering behind unannounced.

No.

Non.

I looked back at the fire and there was just one grouse, so I didn't have to choose.

Il n'y a qu'un seul.

No, monsieur. Regarde encore. Deux grouse. Un pour vous et un pour votre ami.

The man-who-used-to-be-Jim was no longer there.

Where is my friend? Où est-il allé?

I don't know, monsieur. He is your friend, not mine.

But you have seen him before, correct? C'est vrai?

That is not my problem, monsieur.

Tell me, si vous plait, what does my friend look like?

Bien sur, monsieur. You know the answer…. I go now, pour apporter votre salade.

And the maître d', in his white shirt and striped vest, marched away with indignation. According to Jim's theory, I would have to tip him more.

Behind him, an empty wind passed through La Maison Rouge…soul-purging, making me feel shell-like and frigid before the quivering fire…while the single grouse receded into nothing because I had cooked it too long…for decades…time funneling around without touching, and feeling more alone than He has ever known, because I wasn't holding on, as I did in Honfleur.

I called out en français, Allô! But they were all gone.

The lights faded; the only lumination came from the eliding fire, the flames themselves frozen into a final undulation.

In that expanding dimness, one person finally did arrive, scurrying with head down and stained cassock no longer visible. I sensed him stooping wraith-like before me…the Russian servant who had no name.

He brought the grouse, which I ate without seeing. And it was magnifique.

A candle, s'il vous plait?

Later, from the darkness into the darkness, he brought me a fine selection of Normandy cheese, an apple tarte, and un café. And to finish—a glass of calvados.

Outside La Maison Rouge, the fog was so thick I couldn't see my car.

Monsieur! You have not eaten your salad!

I kept on walking, ignoring him…smelling the moldy dampness emanating from the fields.

Monsieur, do not drive in this fog. Trop dangereux!

I turned and could not see him. But from his voice, he seemed close.

There is a hotel at the top of the hill, monsieur. Take the footpath. It is easy to follow, even in the fog.

Footpath?

Oui. Through the field…you will come to a long driveway. Follow it up the hill. There will be a light, monsieur. They always leave a light on.

Where is this path?

You are on it, he whispered, his French body nearly touching mine, Ca va bien. Ca va bien…. His voice not so much ceasing as fading into the sickening fog.

I expected that he had lied. But I was already on the path, the only visible thing inside the darkening pitch of night. *May have to smell my way along.*

Figured I could get my car and suitcase in the morning. I only wished I had a second calvados for the journey. Un autre, s'il vous plait! Un autre….

X

Bonsoir…avez-vous une chambre pour la nuit?

Yes, we can fit you in. One room left.

The man spoke with a clean English accent, but I knew he was really Irish.

That would be grand.

Here is the key…202. Since it's late, we can take care of the details in the morning. You are not traveling with a bag?

I won't be fetching it till morning. My car is at La Maison Rouge. Too much fog to—

I've heard that before. Strange, because La Maison Rouge has been closed for years.

La Maison Rouge? But I just—

You will be quite comfortable here for the night, sir.

The man looked up at me with shy eyes. He was in his early forties…stocky, smooth-faced with short-cropped blond hair. I sensed an air of familiarity about him.

There will be a continental breakfast in the morning, he said, as I headed for the stairs.

D'accord.

The walls and bedspread were lime green; the pillows tubular shaped. I wished I had asked Cal for a toothbrush, because hotels always have extras for folks without their bags. And then it didn't matter, because a primal exhaustion came over me; I fell into the depths…dreaming of not wanting to dream about La Maison Rouge….

And He was there…sitting next to me out of compassion, in the small wooden chair next to my green bed…I knew his presence was a sign of my own weakness, my own failure, and I wanted to repudiate the indignity of him watching me dreaming of Him, with nowhere to flee since I was already at the manoir. And sensing—this would be my last hint of arrival. And He…still ahead of me.

He spoke—

Don't underestimate what I am capable of becoming.

And I—

I was going to say the same thing.

Conspirational voices from the hallway drove him from the chair… footsteps on the stairs, rash noises through ancient walls, the pursuer and the pursued nearly becoming one…trespassing into my room and beyond the other side, onto the green edge of the manoir's midnight light, above the freshly furrowed soil below my window…feeling the vibrations, sensing their hands, his finger…and all the lands surrounding His temporary house crystallizing together until I had to rise up and throw the rock-bird, which He didn't expect from inside his gray slant-away world. So he vanished once more, while I was just moments away from Him. His vestige still present on the simple wooden chair….

In the morning, the desk clerk was an older man—thinner, with gray sideburns and a narrow face. I complained to him about the noises during the night and he, in a French accent—

Impossible! You are the only one staying at the manoir.

But last night, the man who checked me in said the hotel was full…that I had the last room.

That was me, monsieur. I was here when you arrived last night. We talked about your suitcase being in your car, c'est vrai? If you heard things, perhaps it was my wife…. Sometimes she plays night games. She calls it soul chasing. Have you ever done that?

She flitted across the room behind him and into an office. I barely saw her.

Did you say manoir?

Oui, monsieur. This house was once the area's landed manoir. The grand Manoir d'Hermos. We are turning it into a museum, a hotel, and a church.

A church?

Father can explain it to you later, when you return from dinner. There are bagels and coffee waiting for you in the next room. S'il vous plaît.

I turned toward the drawing room.

Pardon, monsieur…. Will you be staying a second night?

Yes. Maybe two.

Si vous souhaitez…take your coffee and bagel and sit in the courtyard out back. It is lovely there.

XI

Would you like fresh coffee?

She approached from behind as I sat at my little metal table.

Yes. You work here?

My husband is the owner.

And your name?

Helene.

She was American and dressed like a waiter with black slacks and a white long-sleeve blouse. Her blondish-brown hair was pulled back in a small ponytail. Her skin was immaculate.

Maybe I will have a chance to meet your husband.

This evening, perhaps.

She smiled with poised lips and then disappeared through a French door into the basement of the manoir. The moment she was gone, I missed her and felt I could love her.

But He was there before me.

I rotated my chair, so I could witness her return.

She carried a cereal bowl with both of her exquisite hands.

Café au lait, she said.

As I picked up the bowl, my fingers were shaking. I needed to eat.

What is the matter with your bagel?

Her green-blue eyes stared through me.

I am sorry....

It doesn't look like something to be eaten?

I nodded.

That's because it is made of plastic, she said.

You understand?

She smiled.

Maybe someone could hang it on the wall, like a piece of art, I joked.

Would you like a cheese omelette?

That would be grand.

Are you Irish?

No.

Why are you talking like one?

I had no response for Helene.

She disappeared into the darkened kitchen, and I slouched in my chair, staring at the line of cypress trees along the property's perimeter. I wanted to put my feet up on the other chair but was afraid she might look out and see.

For the first time since leaving home, I felt peace…as if Pasithea, the Greek goddess of relaxation, had blessed me. Perhaps I was nearer my home than I knew.

Helene returned minutes later with a thin round omelette on a yellow plate. She set it down and handed me a fork. The bagel was no longer there, but I did not remember it going away.

She stood next to me until I took a bite of the omelet, then she sat in the other chair.

When I picked up the coffee, my hands were no longer shaking.

Why are you here? she asked. I don't think you are vacationing.

Helene seemed to have acquired a French accent.

I am trying to find someone.

In Pont-Authou?

I nodded, the bowl of coffee perfectly still in my hands. I had an urge to hold it up high, like a chalice.

You know that this manoir is actually in Thierville?

I didn't…. Does it matter?

I suppose not. I made the same mistake when I came here…. Well, let me know if you find him.

How did you know it was a man?

Allez, monsieur. You know how I know.

She picked up the empty plate and touched my shoulder, her fingers pressing through my flannel shirt into my flesh…and I passed inside the mid-morning slope of sunlight, enveloped by the odor of rosemary and the song of a meadowlark buried in the cypress trees.

XII

From the hallway bathroom window, I could see her sweeping the courtyard three stories below. *And she will meet me in the drawing room…. Es-tu prêt? she will ask. And we will leave the manoir together….*

When I arrived downstairs, the entire manoir seemed deserted.

Under a light rain, I made my descent down the driveway to the path that led to La Maison Rouge. Above my car, half of the sign was broken off, so it read—Maison. Cal was right, the place looked like it had been closed for years.

I peeked into the window and saw the small table and two chairs in front of the fireplace where Jim and I sat…decades ago.

Drove my rental car into Pont-Authou having no idea where to eat. Eventually, I settled on a Basque restaurant because it was well lit and filled with people from the town.

The Basque tradition is communal dining, so I was seated at a long bench among strangers…farmers and ranchers.

No choosing from a menu; the meal was compris. Plates of braised lamb, porc à la crème, veal with mushrooms and peppers arrived at the table. And several carafes of Côtes du Rhône.

When I tried speaking French, they answered in English. I did not tell them my name and did not ask for theirs. There were too many of them. But I did say I was staying at the manoir, and one of the men told me I should have another glass of wine, because I would need it.

Pourquoi? Why?

Ah…he wants to know about the manoir! he exclaimed to everyone.

Someone poured me more red wine before I had finished my glass.

Monsieur, living at the manoir…is a priest and a nun. Well, not really a priest and nun. They are married! For them, c'est possible!

He is Défroqué! said another, making some of them laugh.

Everyone seemed interested in telling me the truth about the manoir.

They say they are fixing it up, monsieur…into a hotel. Mais… the sign in front says *The Church of Yeshua Magdalene*. Have you seen the sign, monsieur? Vous avez vu?

No.

I pushed my plate away. The food was too rich.

Ah, monsieur, you should ask about his church.

And ask him his real name.

Nous savons tous qu'il s'appelle Père M! Father.

Et il n'a pas de prénom? No first name?

Oui.

Non, pas vrai! Son prénom est Francis.

Non, son prénom is Fenton. C'est Fenton!

You should ask him, monsieur. And ask him about défroqué. Defrocked…. For something he did in Northern Ireland. N'est-ce pas vrai, tout le monde? N'est-ce pas vrai? Défroqué! Ireland?

One of the men tried filling my glass again, even though it was still full. I didn't want to hurt his feelings, so I took a big drink.

And she, monsieur…she cannot be a nun. Elle est trop belle. Too beautiful.

And another—

Oui, monsieur. When she appears on the streets of Pont-Authou, all the cars…. Ils se sont arrêter!

A woman in a babushka hit the man in the arm with a broom.

Quelle? he said. C'est vrai! She is—

She hit him again, this time on the back of his head, knocking his hat into the air.

D'accord! D'accord! he hollered, but his words were muffled.

By the time his hat hit the floor, all the women were wearing babushkas and the men, brown hats and large rumpled coats.

The broom fell from her hands.

The man spoke one more time, his mouth remaining still—

The Father…il se cache de quelque chose, monsieur. He is hiding from something.

All of their voices diminished as they resolved into his painting. Not the one composed of brown and green hues, and rugged roiling clouds. But something else….

And I was the only one in motion, my tanned hands edging across the dull oak table, reminding me that I was on the outside. He, allowing me to see as He does.

When they moved again, it was in ancient ways—filling clay jars with dark wine, their tired arms falling into grotesque gestures, begging me to drink. They could not see me, but still they desired to be with me.

Waiters in stained shirts entered and retreated. More carafes of wine appeared without touching hands. Several brooms leaned against the wall—the old-fashioned kind men used to sweep the streets of Paris before the war. Above them, the yellow plaster flaked away…tiny specks floating in the air….

The thick-legged women receded, so the men could be alone with their brooms to dance in tight circles to music I hadn't noticed before, from a Paris music hall, the piano slightly out of tune.

They wanted me to dance with them, but I drank for them instead…for the men lost inside *Dancing with Brooms*, McQuadrian, Pont-Authou, c.1882, while the babushka women faded into the crumbling walls because men so easily forget—the breath of a woman is the center of Being, Jim said…and when a woman dances on a table, the whole world spins on a pin.

A voice broke through—

Come to the ranch with us. It is on the way to the manoir. You have been drinking too much to drive, monsieur.

I knew his name because the others had called him Pasqual.

No, I have to—

Do not worry, monsieur. Someone will bring you home from the ranch.

He patted me on the shoulder, his face close with the vapor of red wine…I had to go with him.

The rain was falling heavy as Pasqual and I ran to his truck. I knew he and the other men were probably larking with me, but I didn't care. Just like I didn't care about the rain. *Let them do what they want.* I expectorated into the night.

I tried to follow the road he was driving on, so I could figure where we were in relation to the manoir. But it was hopeless. Before long, he parked his truck, turned off the headlights, and everything went dark.

C'mon, monsieur. They are waiting for us.

He patted my shoulder like before, so I followed him…my eyes straining downward to identify the puddles.

The men from the restaurant were all there, standing under the eaves of an old wooden barn to avoid the rain. There was a lantern on a tree stump and next to it a pot from which they filled their cups with a ladle.

What are you drinking? I asked.

Baltazaar made it, one of the men said, his hat drooping from the pelting rain so I could not see his face in the lantern light.

Where is he?

Gone. But this is his homemade wine, and we mixed in—

The best French wine! someone yelled.

We mixed in Armagnac. Try it, monsieur…. My name is René.

He loves telling people his name because it means to be reborn! the loud man interrupted.

Heh, hey…he always thinks he is a new man…un nouvel homme!

René ladled me a cup to drink. I looked for Pasqual, but could not see him, so I raised my cup to René—

À votre santé!

To you, too, monsieur, he said, his head down.

I leaned against the barn in the same manner as the other men. Two old rifles rested against the warped wall boards to my left.

After finishing my cup in silence, I walked past the guns toward the corner of the barn.

Oh, monsieur…no need to stand in the rain to piss. There is a toilet in the barn, juste de l'autre côté, other side…this wall. You will see the light.

There was no door, just a filthy toilet and a single yellow bulb hanging by a wire…and a round mirror the size of a dinner plate that looked to be smeared with manure.

The toilet didn't flush. I wasn't surprised because the barn was rank with the smell of urine and rotting hay. I resisted looking into the mirror because it is always a trap…all ontological questions end and the pale reflection is *moonflesh…the neck a breathing stalk with its guilty salience moving even as one swallows for the last time…a long nose from the shoulders up, drifting beyond barriers…make no sound and you are the sound—artery-pulsing rootflesh one second short of expiration…while barely hearing the wooden ladle on the other side of the moldy wall dropping into the cauldron of devil's wine…coming close, nose touching the rusty edge…so no need to move, no need to worry about moving, or to think—I am he and I am He, while all of them try to make me their démon….*

The two shots followed closely upon each other. Felt the pulse of air through the blowhole in the wood behind me, just above my head, before hearing the sound…. In my panic I knew—it was more than one gun.

Ran back through the doorway into the rain. Could see their dark figures standing up the hill about thirty yards from the barn. The two rifles held upright next to them, butt-ends on the ground.

What are you crazy fucking Frenchmen doing? You knew I was inside the barn!

We didn't know, monsieur, the loud one said. Va te faire foutre!

Fuck you, too, I said.

I was closing in on them….

Look, monsieur, now you have been reborn, just like—

René broke in—

I forgot, monsieur. Désolé…. Ces idiots were shooting at the crows.

What crows?

The crows up on the roof, the loud man said. Que pouvons-nous faire? We have been drinking.

The crows of dawn, René added.

Vous êtes des idiots! Dawn is hours away, I yelled.

Yes, but they were already making ehh…. How you say—racket? A lot of noise and…. This is my ranch. My name is Baltazaar, and I can—

They told me you weren't here….

Am I here? Tu ne me vois pas? he said to everyone.

There are no crows, I said emphatically, so close to his face I could almost see him.

On se moquait de toi, monsieur.

The rain was coming down harder.

They will be back. Ils reviennent toujours…. And then you, you can shoot at them. Permet de lui donner a gun.

I have a better idea, René said.

René seemed different, no longer on my side. In the darkness and rain, I could see him for the first time—thin face, mustache, unshaven cheeks, black rimmed glasses.

Where is Pasqual? I demanded.

Probablement…asleep in his truck, René said.

Where is his truck? Où est son truck?

Just one shot, monsieur, Baltazaar said. Then one of us will take you to your manoir.

I don't shoot guns.

One shot…. Then we will be comrades. If there are no birds, just shoot at the barn. C'est ma grange. And I say to you…. Et je m'en fous du tout.

I have a better idea, René said for a second time. Even from here, you can see where Baltazaar missed the rooftop and shot into his own barn. Malheureusement, près de chez vous. Do you see le petit trou. Ah…the tiny hole…where the light is coming through from l'ampoule…the lightbulb…inside the barn. The hole that vous a tellement effrayé….

I shot above his head, said Baltazaar, defending himself. Il n'était pas en danger.

I could see the bullet hole, just a speck of light in the distance.

Yes, tu le vois. You see it, coming through like a ray.

He was right, the light was coming through from the toilet bulb, a faint ray barely penetrating the rain until it was just a glimmer, a small planet…because there was no night sky through the rain, so the night sky was inside Balthazar's barn….

I was freezing, my shoulders shaking. I needed another cup of the Armagnac wine, but dared not walk down the hill with my back to them.

You can shoot at the light hole…where you were, René continued.

Why would I do that?

You will be shooting at yourself, hey hey, Baltazaar broke in. Où tu étais…at the personne you were…tu étais là.

I can see it, but I'm not shooting, I said angrily. I want someone to take me back to the manoir.

And we will, monsieur, said Baltazaar. As soon as you take your shot.... Shoot at the light hole and don't think about...dans un sens...se tirer yourself.

Wait, wait. René said. Il n'est pas chargé.... It is not loaded.

They were ancient single shot bolt-action rifles. Baltazar pulled a bullet form his rain-soaked coat pocket and loaded it in, cocked and locked the bolt, and handed the rifle to me.

Just one shot, monsieur. Ce n'est rien.... It is nothing.

He looked up at me in the rain. I could finally see him—his thick dark hair spreading out beneath his cap, plump cheeks, and his right eye permanently half shut.

Attendez! I said. Check the barn first...see if anyone is in there.

C'est impossible, monsieur. Regarde, we are all here.

Except for Pasqual.

He is in his truck. How do you say...passed out.

C'est bon, monsieur. Go ahead, René said, patting me on the shoulder just like Pasqual.

Another man yelled out--

Baltazaar, crazy as loon...shooting up his own barn!

I fired into the light hole...barely feeling the gun's retort and instead imagining myself still standing in front of the filthy mirror.

Bravo, Baltazaar said. You must have shot through the same hole. There is nothing else.

Unless he missed the barn, said René.

No, he has shot his old self. Now he is reborn, like you, René!

I heard it before I saw it...René hitting Baltazaar across the face with the butt of the other rifle, and then they were both down on the ground. I was glad Baltazaar was in the mud, and Rene too, because he was not my friend. The two other men stood and watched. René kept trying to grab Balthazar's head, crying out, Where are your horns? Putain de démon.... Je vais les attraper et vous entraîner dans la terre!

Where is Pasqual sleeping? Where is his truck? I asked the other men.

Nous ne parlons pas anglais, monsieur.

Merde. Okay.... Où est-ce que Pasqual dort?

René and Baltazaar were still grunting and embracing each other in the primal muck.

Ils vous l'ont déjà dit, monsieur. Dans son camion.

Alors, où est son truck?

The two men approached me in a threatening way, so I held up the unloaded rifle to cross-check them if necessary. René and Baltazaar had both come to rest on their backs, faces staring up into the endless rain.

Where? Où est Pasqual's truck? I demanded again.

They stopped short.

Derrière la grange, où il la stationne toujours.

He works for me, Baltazaar mumbled from his mud hole. Parfois…he sleeps in his truck, sometimes in the barn. Why do you care? Va te faire foutre. Ce n'est pas grave.

I just shot at the barn, you imbécile! And you said—

Baltazaar sat up, his hands in the mud behind him, and spoke menacingly, Il ne comprendra jamais. He doesn't understand, American fool. Crétin!

I walked down the hill toward the barn, still holding the unloaded rifle in my hand. If they decided to shoot at me again, they would only have one gun.

Where are you going, monsieur? To look for Pasqual? He sleeps… like death. Comme la mort, monsieur…. Comme la mort!

I ignored them and walked on.

Pasqual's red truck was behind the barn. I opened the door and the interior light came on—Pasqual was not there. I entered the barn through the back door. The toilet light was no longer on, so nothing but blackness. I moved ahead anyway, feeling in my pocket for matches and that's when I tripped, my body cast headlong into the damp hay. The rifle lost in the darkness.

It was Pasqual! He had tripped me. I patted down his body and found his head. His eyes were closed but I could hear him breathing. I was unsure, though, if he was drunk-asleep or if I had shot him. I tried to wake him, shaking his body and feeling him everywhere for a wound.

You bastards! I screamed and shook Pasqual's body more violently.

Not to worry, monsieur. He always sleeps like that. As lucky as your shot was, you did not hit him.

René stood in the doorway, silhouetted by the light coming from Pasqual's truck cabin.

Il sera bien, monsieur. His name, Pasqual, means Easter.... Like you and I, he will be reborn.

You are all fucking crazy.... Putain de fou!

We are Basques, monsieur. You will never understand.

I thought about being back in my green bed...not caring anymore about the voices and people on the stairs. Soul-play, the manoir clerk called it.... The priest and his nun-wife, whom I loved before he did.

Headlights appeared just beyond the barn door, approaching closer and stopping next to Pasqual's truck. I stood and tried to see through the white glare. I walked out to get a better look. It was a sedan, the passenger door opened....

Get in. I will take you home, said the man-who-was-not-Jim.

I did not talk to him. And I didn't want him talking to me, because I dreaded what he might say.

The rain lightened as we headed around the barn and up the driveway. I could easily see Baltazaar and the other two men still standing on the hillside.

It's a good thing we are getting out of here, Jim said. Those fuckers are crazy! Shooting at their own barn.... Who does that?

I gazed at Jim...sitting solidly behind the wheel of his old Citroen. Jim was a rock...his large-featured face vaguely glowing from the pallid dashboard light. And everything was as it always had been.

XIII

They were both there...lounging on opposite ends of the red-flowered couch in the drawing room. He looked downward and

I knew the problem was my muddy shoes. So I removed my shoes and left them by the manoir's massive front door.

He was African, wearing a chalk-colored chemise that covered his knees, his hair in long braids. She, Middle-Eastern. Hair also in braids. And wearing the same chemise.

Sit, they both said.

And I did…on a hard-backed chair across the room and tried to forget I was wet and cold.

How do you see us? he asked.

He spoke without an accent. And I sensed he could switch into any language he wanted on a whim, and then I would know nothing.

As emanations.

You realize it is you who has allowed us to—

Yes.

Well…. Then you don't have to worry about McCuade anymore.

But—

Stop. If you understood, you would know that McCuade is nothing. He was made—

He snorted a short laugh and continued.

He was a way…to get you here.

Yes.

So you do understand.

His words ceased. And McCuade, who had hitherto been the core of my being, floated away…a filament-self, drifting into the ether.

Would you like a Calvados? she asked.

Before I could answer, she was pouring me a glass from a bottle on top of the gray stone mantel.

Or would you like another café au lait, like I made you this morning?

When I didn't answer, she handed me the Calvados and remained close, her soft chemise touching my hand.

Do you know what we are doing here?

Perhaps.

You are the philosopher. And you don't see—He and I, correcting the lies of the millenia?

That's Nietzsche! You are simply—

No, she commanded.

She walked across the room, lifted her drink from the mantel, and glowered at me. I wasn't sure if she was ridiculing me or about to toast me.

Nietzsche was a prophet, but he did not invent the words. He uncovered them...uncovered the truth about the lies.... Buried because—

She stopped the moment I stood up. After draining my Calvados, I placed the empty glass on the mantel next to hers. Surprisingly, I felt more sober than I had in hours, in years....

She smiled and I felt my ankles weaken inside my wet socks.

You are speaking words that I could have been thinking.

Of course, she said. But aren't you still curious about the mysteries?

With that, they both receded and only her voice remained—

Asherah set him free, your so-called Lord...from his lonely castle, his lonely god-dom...Asherah, older than Yahweh because He descended from El. And Asherah, El's consort before being His...until Babylon, when the post-exilic Jews needed to know why Yahweh had forsaken them yet again, and came to believe that it was Asherah who was in their way...to Him. Yahweh himself commanding the destruction of her shrines to maintain the purity of their worship of Him.... And so She, the greatest apotheosis of sexuality and power, elided away, and they knew only Him...with the Hebrew priests pretending that She had never been, and the ancient patriarchs secure in the fact that men would grow to fear a mono-god, to believe that Yahweh was suigeneris, that He was solus ipse...and that He alone gave birth to existence by proclaiming Let There Be.... Their words, not His...and the Jews became the only people on Earth to believe in a universe generated without Her...forgetting, as well, that before everything was, She IS.... And in their holy writings, despite all their patriarchal fantasies, She is still encoded, waiting...for the lies of the millenia to be vanquished....

But you already knew all of this, she said, standing next to me once more. The greatest lies—what has been left out. Not just about Yahweh, but about Yeshua, no longer to be called Jesus....

...And Magdalene His lover, His consort...before the Holy Roman Apostolic transformed her into a sinner, as Luke said—to anoint His feet and seek repentance...Magdalene, who traveled with Yeshua, knowing Him in a way they never did...before Paul turned Him into a Man only among men, and the early church subjugated women in His name...with the priests' celibacy draining Magdalene for centuries... of her sexuality, her power, her Being...and the lies of the millennia... until her Gospel was found and Magdalene finally had a voice—What is hidden from you I will proclaim, she said. And Peter—The Savior made you worthy, who are we to reject you? He loved you more than us.

Are you still thinking of Nietzsche? she asked, her hip touching mine through her chemise.

Why?

Because then you would miss the reconjoining.

Père and Helena, Asherah and Yahweh, Magdalene and Yeshua...blessed by their new church...through one priest and one nun, sacred coition, reprogenerating.... All.

This isn't Nietzsche, I said.

They arose up from the sofa together.

We hope you enjoyed your evening in Pont-Authou, he said.

And she—

We go to capture sleep, before the crows of dawn.

She took his hand and led him toward the stairs. They ascended slowly, until it seemed they were one Being.

I'll stay up a bit longer, I said.

But they didn't hear me.

I moved to the couch and slouched backward, not caring about getting the cushions wet. After a few minutes I dozed off....

XIV

The crows of dawn awakened me. Their rattling caws…disjunctioning all.

The cacophony increased as I mounted the stairs, pausing on the landing.

They must be on the rooftop.

The birds ceased the moment I reached the second-floor hallway that was dark, except for the dim light coming from the stairs. My room was at the end, next to the bathroom. *An easy distance to achieve.*

Halfway there, a door on my right edged open from a surge of wind and I turned to see droplets of spectral light cascading downward through the darkness.

The rushing air was an updraft from her widening feathered wings…etching slowly into vision…illumined by their collision with the celestial sparks.

I could smell the animal glory of her muscular wings. And I marked her long feathers shading from black to silver white.

By childhood volition, I stepped into the room, remembering how I had confessed to Sister Helen in fifth grade—*I love you and want to marry you, Sister…when I am older. If you will wait for me. And she, in her Irish accent, you are a silly boy if you don't know nuns can't marry, except to Jesus. If you have enough love for God, she said, you could be His emissary, His blood in life, His priest. Oh yes, I said. Then as a priest I will marry you. And she—priests and nuns can't marry either, my sweet boy. But, Sister, in the Church of Jesus Magdalene in France, they can. There is no church such as that, she replied with impatience. There is, I said. A man sleeping behind the rectory wall told me so. And he looked just like a saint, Sister. Just like a saint. That's impossible, she said. But I saw him, Sister. And that means we could live together in France, Sister. If you will wait for me….*

His legs were still and useless as She rose higher into the lotus-smelling dark.

Moments later, the interspersed air had the odor of onycha, forbidden incense of the gods, which I remembered breathing once before….

I am with her. And not with him.

And I am she and I am he.... Before everything, was I....

With her animal wings, because Sister Helen had waited for me. And She is upon me, amid a swirling smoke of myrrh, until there is nothing else...inside the luminous margin where near-gods mingle with mortal flesh...my weakening hands drifting across her sharp shoulders, my closed eyes seeing without seeing, but sensing her tongues of fire across my paling skin. I heard voices...*Donegal, Inishtrahull, Pont-Authou.... And an angel wrote the words of Him who holds the seven stars...with a trumpet voice calling me to come hither...to show me what must take place after this, after the white garments and golden crowns torch into fire...and before me a sea of glass, like crystal, to which I must return.*

I know I must return.

Where?

To Soda Lake....

For what?

Who was that?

Before everything was, She is....

While for some it is the flange and the rail, for others—Heraclitean Fire....

And Pasithea, goddess of consciousness, visits without knowing, so there is no witness....

And our eyes reversed, are like snares, blocking the freedom of her going....

And Her world—never nowhere-without-end....

And no soul-scalping, when the winds take forests in their paws....

And no eliding, from the double voices we hesitate to hear....

And no missing the uniform hieroglyph, sprouting in broad zones... missing one place, appearing another, where He will be waiting....

And no turning into other selves before She descends in glory from the darkening blue into the fire....

While the sparrows speed down aslant the black world, the bright air trembling at the heart of their pulse....

And no forgetting the moments that cannot be communicated, and never repeating them....

And no asking—why am I in this place? astride the grave where nothing survives the profusion of darkness....

And no fearing the fusty Almighty, who hurls headlong flaming from the ethereal sky with combustion down to bottomless perdition... all messianic souls....

Saying these words, because He knows I love them....

And Heraclitus...shliberish of tongues...shblankton in holberloo, en plankosh ferbotkin, inselmaflog der blehrbuskatof du errman sanctum....

And no more Here Comes Everybody, again...as the Ancient of days, McCuade, raises himself up once more. Because no one can do it like he does, so no one knows, or hears—in Inishtrahull in spiritus I am, אני...in sula rahib, gach ruda aragosama...ansin in Acaill I gcónaí....

While before his eyes all youth fades into specter selves....

Dogs in her eyes, so weary...the lass of Connemara....

The droplets of spectral light ceased; the weight and rank of her wings upon me no more.

And the icon of Mary, along with her piecemeal dove, swept from the corners of our eyes....

The room is vacant. The bed undisturbed. The smell of the damp gray air has returned.

I continue down the paling corridor, past the door to my room, into the bath.

I have already packed my things. Jim is taking me to the train station in the morning. It is time to leave the manoir.... McCuade will not be going with me.

The sun had not yet set when I threw my old boots over the balcony. They landed in the neatly furrowed field below. A mist of dark soil arose and then dispersed. The boots lay solid, engraved there.

In the morning, the boots will be gone. And Jim will see an old French man wearing them down the streets of Pont-Authou. McCuade will see that, too. Because there is a time to finish knowing. Just then...whether I created McCuade, or if he created me, in order for Him to come into being.

The bulb above the bathroom sink is not working. In the dusk light, I withdraw from the mirror like she would. Helena—blazoning within me.

At a small metal table she served me an omelette and confessed—He put the god-thing in me. Soon, she said, I will put the god-thing in him.

And Yahweh, at the beginning of time, all-gendered.... And Asherah, there before He knew Her....

From the courtyard below, piercing through the layers of twilight, the voice of a young girl. I recognize her when she calls my name. But her presence seems distant and fractured. Yet she is there...just beyond the fading line of cypress trees that edge out the limits of time.

Where is papa? she asks.

He is on his way, a voice replies.

The bathroom window is painted shut and will not open.

But Jim is repairing the manoir; soon all the windows will open.

I yell anyway, believing she will hear me through the glass.

I am on my way! I am on my way down to the courtyard....

Chapter Ten
ACHILL ISLAND

I

Took a swim today. Thought it would be my last.

Ah, but I always think that. Was saying such to Sean last night. He was smoking a fag on the front steps of the Achill Head. Talking again about proper weather.

Only Achill has proper weather, he says. Sean…looking a bit like I used to.

But never mind that….

Walked past the old Cyril Gray house in the early evening. Edifice clotted with moss and mold. Thought I could hear his wife's thin voice from inside the crumbling plaster. But then I passed right by her, sitting in a wheelchair outside the front door of her stone row-house, staring up into the damp oak leaves, purple shawl around her neck. Dogs in her eyes. So weary….

I kept on walking. Don't think she noticed me.

Years ago, she asked if I would oblige her. No thank you, I said. But I appreciate the offer. Then fook-off down the road with you, she said. So I went on my way.

Could barely see the Silver Strand in the consuming twilight. Lovely to bathe there. Be careful about the rips, everyone likes to say. But I've never been caught in one. Not a boley Irishman like myself!

Good to be out…not having to bother with his cloying presence inside the cottage. *His white cottage by the sea*, he likes to say. But only for a little while.

On the third day, he is talking to himself. What does it matter, he thinks, I'm here alone. Exhausting for me, though.

Don't know why I haven't left him, especially since he believes I'm already gone. Coming on five years, it is.

Hard listening to him...thinking he is nothing but himself. And the more he talks to others, the more he imagines he's becoming Irish.

The cottage was warm when I returned. Didn't trust it, though. When he gets back, he will fuss with starting a peat fire. Then give up.

For him, the rituals consume...the quotidian washing of his face, the regimen of changing clothes, the nervousness about the weather.... Sometimes he doesn't get up until the afternoon. Still feeling like he hasn't slept. Avoiding the sledge of having to write about someone he has lost faith in...wanting to believe it was I, not he, who gave.... But not I is what he hears.

A flawed man...who understands more about the dead than he knows. How they see differently. Whispered that to him one time.

His voice from the front door. He's back from having heroic pints with his lads.

He'll put on music, pour himself a Paddy, and peruse his notes spread across the kitchen table. Sense of order is what he likes. Then, seeing through it for a moment, he remembers....

Angry he is tonight. Talking to himself in a raised voice. Rare chance for it—inside a dwelling alone. Calling out to me; cursing me. And I am right here, if he could feel his own voice.

When he dances to the jazz, I will leave. I *can* leave.... Will not stand for him watching his reflection in the night window, thinking it is I.

Still has the lanky frame of a boy, moving pretty well...his gray hair waving upward, beyond the outline of the darkened window. He seems to like it. Slight smile.

I'm going to fucking do this! he exclaims loudly. And we know what he means. But not sure he believes it. *I'm fooking doing it right now*, he would say to me if he could. Convincing enough to make me wonder....

His mood is up in the late night. His time, he likes to say. And indeed, it is. Not much skin of mine.

The jazz is laced with children's voices, distorting into a primal whine. Whose children are they? The music of heaven, he wants to believe. Then he says the words softly—*the music of heaven*. As if his mother might hear.

Takes a drink of his whisky, lights a cigarette. Returns to his dancing.

I am leaving....

He *is* the music. Happy for now. Forgetting his anger about the many days of rain and not writing. Well, just a few lines...an image of an old lady in a wheelchair, purple shawl coiled about her neck, staring blankly at the trees and listening for the dripping of the leaves. He doesn't know what kind of trees they are. Will have to ask the caretaker. No matter, he will make them oak trees. Easy enough. And it is.

His mind will spiral until after two, then cease. And there will be peace in the Achill Cottage.

As he sleeps, he believes he can hear the dry bog-land draining into Blacksod Bay.

When he dreams, his mother will be calling to him. But not what he expects.

Come, she says. Even though you were the last born, you could be the first to leave.

Now why would that wonderful woman say that?

She disappears around a corner wall. I do not know when she will return.

II

Saw Sean at the Valley House playing a bit of guitar. Admire the fact Sean can do so many things—builder of boats, teacher of children...Sean asked me to sing. The ballad about the lass from The Rosses lost in the fog and storm. But I declined. Don't want folks having to pretend my voice is better than it is. Bought Sean a pint just the same.

He sat himself at the corner of the bar and patted Sean on the back. Wants Sean to think he's a good ol' lad. Tells the bartender, Julian, a thin Frenchman, about his reading at the Valley House. Next week, it is. And he better not read about me…some lie from the ganglia myth of who he thinks I am. Would not dare do that… not to a boley Irishman like—

Do you know what room it will be in?

The old dining room, Julian says.

The grandest structure on the island—the Valley House. And no one forgets the awful business with Agnes MacDonnell in 1894, at the hands of that scoundrel—James Lynchehaun. Strong, dark-souled man. Animal-like. And Synge made high art of it. But that's too much to go into now….

III

He's been out having a pint with the caretaker, Mr. John S. A fine Irishman.

Pours a whisky and, before I can anticipate, screams—*I can't fucking do this! Not without…. Where are you, McCuade? You bastard… I figured out the lies of Pont-Authou. I get it now…. Why he said you were nothing. And now believing—you are older than They.*

Older and unwritten…. Until I….

It was all You, from inside of them.

The music comes on. A soul refrain—like a king, like a king, like a king…. Told him about Ben H years ago. And now the music is his.

He dances and looks into the night window. He is uneven, without joy. Through the reflection inside the dark glass, he does not see himself. He is concerned; his jaw-line shifts. Then he does…. Through an aphotic layer of the sun, he thinks—it is I.

Then I is gone.

IV

Out with his lads again. Young bartenders from the island. Me lads! he calls them.

After The Amethyst closes, they cross the street to The Annexe Inn. He sits on the porch with Rearrie, watching Kieran fight with Rory over the pool table. They barrel through the door onto the porch, and through the second door to the outside. The pub owner, short unhappy woman, chases them with a broom. Moments later it is over and the lads are all sitting on the porch rolling cigarettes.

Kieran rolls one for him. Licking it pretty well at the end. Sniffling, Kieran is. He worries about putting the wet cigarette into his mouth. But Kieran is watching him, so he does.

Do you have a cold? he asks.

It's nothing, Kieran says, dismissing the air with his bruised left hand. Will jump into the sea tomorrow. Cure for everything.

Kieran gives him a light and he tastes the sickness. Breathes it in.

Two a.m. He leaves.

Good night, lads! he exclaims as he turns to look for his car in the dark.

V

Prescient about getting sick. Miserable, he is. The only man to have a cold.

Beyond his window, skinny-legged sheep trot up the street and the gray afternoon mesmers on....

Listening to the rain since a moment ago. Listening, for so many years....

Half asleep, he doubts I am here.

Unprepared, he is...to believe I am.

Convinced he's at the edge, cliffs of frightfall....

Alone and ill in a foreign land. And when he dreams, voices defeat him. Better to be up and about! Like a boley Irishman, glowering into the gray light….

Talking to himself, he is. And I tire of listening. Sometimes he records it, imagining I hear.

VI

McCuade! Come out.

Are you still seeing everything?

And I believed you were no more…. Fool I was, to make of you what….

McCuade!

More than a man…. Oh, I remember…. The essence of all one imagines him to be….

Imagines her to be. That's it, isn't it? Himher, to be…until breathing itself feels like something….

Out of the shocking Empyrean, He appeared…first child of the Absolute. Is that how you think of yourself?

Out of the sky-smoldering superannuation, They appear…before the names of all the gods and daemon were known….

McCuade! You son of a bitch! Where are you?

Not yet time-worn, are ye?

Realizing just one thing…knowing just one thing….

Break loose from the echelons!

What was that? Who was that?

More than a man. More than himher. Envisioning herhim….

Is…the greatest word. More ancient than Yahweh, McCuade is's onward….

Older than them all. More human…more honest, more clever, more dangerous, more playful….

Just once, to hear your voice…. And then I will read you aloud, inside the house that arose from the primal valley, during the endless adoration warfare….

Hearing the voice of Him, feeling his shapeless breath...from me, to me, within me.... And He is...there!

[Recorded September 9, 2018, 1:30 a.m. Achill Island]

VII

Going to visit the lads in the daylight at the Valley House. Stops on the Dugort Road to give a tired-looking girl a ride. She is staying at the Valley House hostel. Confesses to being an artist, but doesn't know what she wants to create.

At the Valley House, the lads are deep in the Irish muck, digging trenches under a steady rain. Hired by the owner, Rory's uncle, to put in new plumb lines. The lads work to pay for their drink.

Kieren no longer has his cold. Cured, he claims, by swimming in the sea. Jumped off a rock at the end of a secret path from the Valley House.

They assure him they will be there on September 12.

What are you reading? Rearrie asks.

Not sure yet, lads.

But he knows.... Knows and is afraid to say.

On his way out, gazes once more at the faded posters on the courtyard wall, detailing the story of Agnes MacDonnell and James Lynchehaun. Obsessed, he is, with the dark Irish tale. *The Yellow Lady and the Achill Outrage / The Big House is on Fire! / Edward VII vs James Lynchehaun / Agitation on Achill—Police and People in Conflict.*

All subsumed by Synge into his notorious drama—The Playboy of the Western World.

Gets into his car, heads back to the cottage. Considers going for a run in the rain.

VIII

Lunch at The Beehive. Grilled chicken panini.

Sitting with a book. Determined not to look at the flyer in the window. Him, it is. But the face stares past him.

Reading at the Valley House, Achill, County Mayo. 8:00 p.m. And in orange lettering across the top—*All are Welcome!*

Sets him thinking about Kafka, and his unfinished novel—*Amerika*...a dream-fantasy. Release from the dreariness of Prague, the only place Kafka ever knew. Never traveling farther than France, but projected an America of the mind, with Karl Rossmann marching off at the end into the Nature Theatre of Oklahoma where "all are welcome."

Reverie ceases. Decides not to finish the panini. Stands up. Doesn't move. Lost, he is.... Stares at the photo. Can't remember when it was taken. Knows it was by a creek, captured by a Mr. Eric J.

The photo reveals nothing. Achill has changed him. No one on the island knows. They simply expect him to appear.

The lads will be there, and others...Francis and Ham....

He saw Francis the other day at his Red Fox Press.

Wish I could build a peat fire like you, he said.

On a piece of parchment, Francis drew for him—the architecture of fire.

Francis, grand behind his desk. An elder-god...slightly stooped, gray beard, long gray hair swept behind his ears. Deep watery eyes. No one gazes too long.... Edges of the universe are there.

Born in Bruges. And his female love, Antic-Ham, born in Korea. She, always with her wide-brimmed hat. Spanning the globe, they ever-be...emanating into each other as the Eternal Artist...designing and printing, in their white cottage on a cliff above the sea.

From Achill, they can alter the world's gravitational pull. He has felt it. They do not, because they are inside it...where hammers hang from the thatch eves, just beyond the arc of time.

Hand-silking the books of the ages, while their peat fire neither expands nor contracts. The flames inextinguishable...undulating with the rhythms of the Earth and born from Achill's ancient bogs.

I will come by your cottage and show you how to burn the peat, Francis says.

Thanks. I can figure it out.

But he won't. Embarrassed, he is…yet somehow still knowing, without understanding, that when he is with Francis and Ham, he is close to me.

What? He's already left The Beehive?

IX

Visiting his friend, James, chef at the The Bervie. Wanting help with his computer. James knows what he's doing but doesn't have the time. Too busy at The Bervie. So much on the young man's shoulders…preparing the best dinner on Achill.

A gracious thank you and goodbye to James, whom he hugs to feel the Irish.

Still enough light for a drive to Keem…remote, blue-flag beach of the gods. Horseshoe-shaped, golden, Keem is visible from Croagh Patrick. So pristine, Patrick declared—*no one will ever drown there.* And no one has.

He knows the story, but does not believe.

His wetsuit on, he considers going in. But he is alone, and the rain is falling again. He will not swim in the rain. Beneath the darkening, he is not a boley….

X

What ho? Already back from the pubs?

Filled with regrets, he is. The writing…the only reason he is here. And he won't look at the first pages, even though I want him to.

Has uncovered something. But sees nothing. Will blame it on me. That bastard McCaude.

As if he ever—What?

His reading tomorrow night. Still doesn't know. And can't find his way without—

XI

I am not going to call out for you anymore. I don't have to...because I have figured out before you ever knew. Millennia ago....

More than a man...greater than Yeshua, than Asherah and Magdalene...than Yahweh...I heard you say or heard me say....

Askance the spheres and the strings, you sweet son of a—

Greater than ergo sum, McCuade Quidditas interspersed the land, fathered and mothered where I being said yes...past the groaning moment, beyond the terrible infinite...gray-blue heshehewas, shblankton in holberloo, en plankosh ferbotkin...I can speak that, too, without knowing the words. And you don't want me to read at the Valley House...because him almighty could hurl headlong flaming—gigerabush wafers ethereal....

Disintegrating evenly, the shadow-selves mix, while the others fritter away....

Will never mourn you, though I may still dance in the window to catch a glimpse of you. Knowing who you are, you will know who I am and they will know us for the first time—scio ego, qui sum usque in sempiternum.... Je sais qui je suis pour toujours....

Before everything was, McCuade infinito...revealed through the darksome valley burn....

Now Appearing! All are Welcome!

[Recorded September 11, 2018, 2:04 a.m. Achill Island]

XII

Not finished yet, he is. But can't figure him. Something altered from what he was.

Remember his moaning one night—I want Achill to fucking change me!

Thinks he failed at that, but only in the manner he imagines.

XIII

He is less present now when he fades away. And we are barely one when he is gone.

XIV

He records again. Don't need to hear his words. Any fool Irishman can listen.

Pathetic, the yelling—*You need me!*— Believing he understands for the first time.

For you to exist…. No otherwise knowing.

Palaver…churned from Hegel's worn-out notions. His *Absolute Idea*. Hegel needing to write those words before universal consciousness could begin. I remember…the obfuscated German narcissism, the Allemandes Abstraktionen! And the end of desire begins…followed by the dissolution of the old gods.

But not you! Monsieur McCuade, Monsieur Maquadrian, Monsieur………

[Stops recording.]

XV

I hear your voice, that is what has changed. A voice no one ever….

So is it I who am solis ipse. I who am the voice.

Before everything was, I voice….

Finally out of the way of myself. First time—hearing being....

His being heard before I being McCuade Dominus.

Believes he has accepted what he's almost realized. Unsure whether to read about us at Valley House...where someone might imagine—He is there!

He records again—

McCuade! It will be okay...McCuade?

Expects me to answer. Absurd possibility—hearing what he imagines my voice to be...the essence of all one imagined McCuade to be....

His words trying to find mine.

His words not mine.

Stops recording.

I got it! he exclaims. I fucking got it!

XVI

He plays the jazz. The great Mr. John Coltrane. Thinks he is a god.

Pours a glass of Paddy. The routine resumes. But something else....

Speaks like he is recording, but he is not.

Ever since Donegal...I have been missing.

Missing?

It has been your story all along, hasn't it? Always your story.... So why not your words?

Your voice I hear...of you watching me.

So you will do the telling, because you always have.... That's it, isn't it? That is what I hear—

His voice from the front door. He's back from having heroic pints with his lads. He'll put on music, pour himself a Paddy, peruse his notes spread across the kitchen table. Sense of order is what he likes. Then, seeing through it for a moment, he remembers....

Sounding like you.... Hearing beyond seeing.

He lights a cigarette. Paces.... Thinks about dancing. Something holding him back. Avoids the night window; afraid it will fail-looking.

Switches to Beethoven. The Seventh Symphony. The majestic opening...nearly a sonata in itself.

Pours another Paddy.... When the second melody comes on, he moves toward the night window.

He conducts into the dark recesses of the glass. I watch him from the other side. Through the tortured reflection, with eyes closed, he sees me.

His thin ageless hands rise in sacrificial pose, his crest of gray hair slightly waving. The center of his narrow face—the equitime point of the universe.

As the threnody of the second movement begins, He mourns.

From the fading corners of his eyes—the primal anguish of all time. The Allegretto...composed His whole life. This symphony—His greatest toil.

Are you Dasein? I ask. That's it, isn't it?

But the Heideggerian stitching is too easy. Still, I love Dasein.

Outside, the sheep are on the move. Up the road, they trot, their blown-up bodies and stick-thin legs advancing. Their eyes unembarrassed...staring with indifference beneath their useless horns.

From the inside, I can see Him anytime I want. He is free, and I...trapped by everything He once was.

Drinks my whisky. Thinks about dancing. Nothing holding him back.

Smiles knowingly...because He loves all that I have loved—the novels of Woolf, the wisdom of Du Bois, the vision of Blake, the poetry of Dickinson, the philosophy of Kierkegaard...the sacrament of swimming....

XVII

Feeling all myself again. Moving about the cottage at will. Freeness of Being.... Nearly erotic, it is.

Would like to see Sean tonight. Smoke a fag with him on the steps of the Achill Head. Talk about his music and proper weather.... Only Achill has proper weather, he says.

Sean...looking a bit like I used to. But never mind that....

And he will recognize me as he wants to see me.

XVIII

My sister is coming after all. Arriving in Westport on the train, just in time for the reading.

Worries her brother is going mad...alone in his cottage by the sea.

Not madness, I will tell her. Just that bastard McCuade.

He will be leaving Achill soon....

Saw a tinkerer the other day. Don't often see them on Achill Island. Dragging his cart up the Slievemore Road. Seemed to be carrying a corpse...covered with a baby's blue blanket. Smelled it... the sickly sweet effluvium.

Could have been me, drudging my rough cart with McCuade's head dragging behind in the furrows. But McCuade smells of nothing. Even Yeshua smelled...rank with a carpenter's sweat. I remember that.... But McCuade—composed or decomposed, smells of nothing. Divine nothingness.

XIX

My sister arrives at the station. Her eyes cloudy. We hug, both of us slump-shouldered.

Excited to see the cottage, she is. But little time. The reading is at eight.

Light rain falling as we drive up the rutted road to the Valley House. Me lads stand inside the dusk-lit picture window. Rearrie tips his cap. Kieran smirks and hails me with his glass. My sister knows there is much to figure out.

Francis and Ham are there, Jim from the Bervie, the artist-girl who walks Dugort Road, and the leaders of the Heinrich Böll Foundation....

A Guinness awaits at the lectern, where a single lamp shines. The rest of the room will abide beneath the descending darkness of West Ireland.

And the nimbus of time is wherever He is...on Achill Island.

The director—an adroit, bespeckled woman—introduces him. Highlights accomplishments from his resume. The lads enjoy hearing all he has become.

The faces in the room are pasted into place...all the people he has known over the last month.

He reads from an earlier book, knowing within minutes that he is missing them—

But Taddy Keegan was already gone. And I was almost too late to see, except for the last dark shape of him against the brightness, his arms still above his head through the downfall sunlight into the Allegheny River that looked black and distant under the noon sky.

He stops. Drinks his Guinness. Reaches for the leather satchel and his mind shifts away...voices in the worn hallway, voices on the stairs...fire burning atop the courtyard walls. And Agnes MacDonnell dead. Heraclitean fire, it was.

He falters and leans...almost out of it. Once there, no coming back.

His voice begins again.

Something closer to home for you. About a man.... No, more than a man.... The essence of all one imagines Him to be.... The essence of something we call Mc—.

Ecclesiastical trespass to speak of him!

Your insane apostasy has nothing to do with me.

His words disturb the atmosphere—his sister shifts in her chair. The director jousts at her eyeglasses. The lads' teeth widen.

A few years ago, I went in search of him. A spiritual quest, perhaps...to get to the idea beyond the idea.... Was informed by a man who slept outside my garage. Said He was the only man he ever loved. And that He had returned to Donegal. But my search led me farther north, to Malin Head. And then beyond...to Inishtahull Island, an abandoned two-billion-year-old metamorphic rock. Conveyed there by a fisherman named Jeremiah. That is all true.

He removes the manuscript from his satchel and time ceases. Then begins again when he sips his Guinness. After setting the glass down, he gazes at the audience, memorializing their faces.

His hands fuss with the pages before settling beneath the lamp. The rest of the room is ensconced in twilight. He lifts his voice and the pages fritter away...like feathers from Icarus's wings, and there are only his fallen words—

The rain started up again, for the final time, so loud I couldn't hear anything except his low humming voice inside the raw dampness of the house, like ancient white noise that only I was attuned to recognize.

I am ready, I wanted to say aloud.

He is not.

WHAT WAS THAT? Nietzsche asked about the corporeal life of Jesus. And the apostles, after Jesus's death, wondering—WHO WAS THAT?

The rain had receded forever. So that I could hear his footsteps on the green-soaked moss just beyond the door.

Coming to visit?

Could not see him seeing me.

McCuade, is that you? I yelled across the darkness.

And in that very moment, His voice withdrew...through the walls of the Valley House, across Lough Nambrack toward The Silver Strand. No excruciating tearing apart, just a draining away beyond the limits of being. And the simultaneous sadness of him-no-more-with-me.

Turned on my flashlight and climbed out the window, determined to see what was there. Walked through the damp high grass around the cottage, but couldn't find him.

Could he have gone inside the house while I was looking for him outside?

So I went back toward the window, and that's when I heard him calling from inside his stone house—

McCuade, come inside!

He is calling himself now. How cunning of him.

Draining away, he is…like the dry bog land into Blacksod Bay.

Though the rain had stopped, I was still damp to the bone. So I went back inside and wrapped myself in the blankets again and took out my notepad. For the first time, McCuade was one step behind, so I need to write everything down, I decided.

> *All quiet now….*
>
> *Would love some water.*
>
> *There is an old cistern between Portmore Landing and McCuade's house, but the water inside is bacteria ridden. That's why he has trained himself not to drink when on Inishtrahull.*
>
> *Nearly 3:00 a.m. Heard a noise in the corner. One of the rats. Put my flashlight on to look for him, but they are too quick to see. No more sitting on the ground with the rat moving about. So I sat on the chair, my damp coat still hanging off the back of it, and wrapped the blankets around my legs. I must look like a vagrant.*
>
> What the hell has happened to you?
>
> *A slight sound on the outside of the door. Scratchy, like tiny claws. If someone wants in, they should just use the empty window. Reluctantly, I turned on my flashlight and stuck my head out the window again.*

Is anyone there?

Damn this!

But the "damn this" came at me from behind. He was in the house somewhere. I shined the flashlight around. Nothing in the room but the chair, the old fireplace, the two books and candles, and broken pieces of a wooden table in the corner….

> *Decided to go outside one final time. Slight breeze. Nothing else but the northern Irish silence. Smell of the sea and passing rain and mossy greenness. Could nourish one for a while…*especially a boley Irishman such as myself! *Kept my eye on the window as I paced before the front of the house. Heard something moving inside. A dragging sound across the stone floor. Poked my flashlight through the window. Nothing.*

Who the hell is there?
The echo of the words resounded behind me.

> *Angry for the first time. Sick of whatever He was….*
> *Hungry and thirsty. Feeling…at my end.*

Still, he believes McCuade is on his way; his boat delayed by the storm.

> *McCuade is here.*

To test him, I stuck my head out the window and yelled—Yoohoo! Then retreated inside to see if I would hear my own voice again calling him, or calling my self. But there was nothing.

> *Conclusion: you can't make yourself hear Him. McCuade has to do the calling and he has to be ready to listen. And that's why everyone except McCuade has left Inishtrahull. And that's why on Inishtrahull, Ireland's northern most island, time loops around like the beam from the lighthouse. Things seem to happen, with some variation, and time passes. But there is no real movement beyond the inside and outside voices, and one is trapped within an unresolved moment. Feeling the texture of time itself passing like shadows from a distant planet.*

The eschatological night has become aphotic.

I have to leave this house and go down to Portmore to free myself from His moment. Someone-not-McCuade will have to bring the boat in.... Jeremiah, after dawn.

But he thinks it will be....

The rain is over, and it won't be any colder at Portmore than inside McCuade's stone house.

XX

The Irish applaud. They love a story they won't forgot to remember.

Your great, great grandfather was a fucking god! he exclaims, his face close.

Thick black eyebrows, gray hair dangling into thin dreadlocks. Wears a jeweled pin on his lapel—a golden Irish harp. His name—Steve.

He notices me staring. Removes the pin and gives it to me.

You should have it, he says.

And talks not of the passing of McCuade, but of a Mr. Denis O who lived from 1695–1807. Northern Ireland's greatest harpist. Your great ancestor, he says. And during the last years of his life, he had a wen on his head and was carried on a cot across Northern Ireland.

Around the corner from the great dining room, the Valley House Pub. Pints with the lads. My sister bucking up, smoking cigarettes in the courtyard with Rearrie. Steve is gone.

When I see Steve again, it is at the cottage, playing my ancestor's songs—mournful beauty transposed to guitar, plucked by two fingers. His eyes closed as he trances the music. Looking a bit like McCuade....

He is familiar with the cottage, knows where the teapot is. Moves like he has lived in the cottage for a thousand years, and I am his guest. After tea, he once more lifts my father's great song for my sister and me to hear.

In the morning, toasting a goodbye glass of Paddy with the caretaker, Mr. John S. Looking a bit like McCuade, he is.

We pause at the gate to wave back at him. Reluctant, I am, to leave Achill Island...where McCuade lives in his white cottage above the sea. From Achill, he is lord and god. And sometimes Helena, looking like Asherah, with her long black braids and golden-brown skin, is with him, and the whole world feels their gravitational pull.

Even from a distance, I can impression Him...reflected through the darkened window.

I close my eyes for as long as it takes to feel the corporeal thread of time unraveling. And when I open them, I see his wavering body, like the shimmering lighthouse itself, moving across the water. Bolted together, they are, beneath the Irish Sea, with the yellow-orange sun flashing off the waves in blinding streaks. McCuade... forever returning out of the infinite darkness from which our imagination fails to rescue Him. And it is...as it always has been.

SODA LAKE

I

i

Crenulated salt dust from last sway of sea.

Crust-face, swollen lips. Nose touching the white-salt edge.

Drifting beyond barriers…

Make no sound and you are the sound.

Artery-pulsing rootflesh with no need to worry about moving or to think—

I am he, and I am He…

ii

I remember all of that…

But I am not Abel. Not mist of the Earth, not vapor, not breath.

So I can rise from the salt dust.

iii

Sailing alone across the white abyss…

Where are the others?

Who is doing the asking?

Perhaps I could draw them together inside a salt courtyard, or dissolve their boundaries before returning through the same footsteps to see who will arrive.

iv

I remember the story about the axe…freeing the lord from his vegetative womb.

And imagining the body rising up before I am able…through the purple-gray ribbons of time…beyond the plaintive sojourners who do not understand their own stories.

Voices on the stairs, fire burning atop the walls…while the mind flickers into dreams He is incapable of dreaming, and that is why He cannot imagine us. So he listens—to the ruse of self, tilting toward it…

vi

When will it be my turn? He wants to know. And I—no longer needing to see Him, after so long imagining Him. Giving him a name. And He, not concerned about the multitude failing to find Him.

Ever bothersome, He overshadows them…who desire to see, rather than to know, Him.

vii

The other voices elide, only he remains. But no dragging him across the salt ice, no removing Him from the story. Until, after a while, it seems there is only Him. Then only me. Then me and him, which will take a millennium…before discovering I have not fallen through the white glass, and open my thin, brown fingers.

II

i

A man stands atop the hill next to his car. Stares in my direction, but cannot see me. Too much distance, and too much distraction—consciousness swirling in the way of thought.

In a moment, he will drive down to the shore of Soda Lake and walk toward me in my footsteps...his feet dropping deeper into the crust the farther he goes.

Still, I cannot see the man. He blends into the shimmering, even with his dark clothes.

ii

The first one lay posed against my garage wall, not yet sleeping.

I remember—the only man he ever loved.

I will find him, I said. And the others followed.

Walking onto the lake, trying to decide how far to go, my feet breaking through the white glass into primal black mud.

Crawling until, so tired, I have to lie down. And he, slowly following but hard to see with the white salt absorbing Him into a glint of sunlight.

iii

I park next to the lake, but can't see the man when I get out of the car.

His footprints—in the salt dust. I step inside them, but sink in deeper the farther I go.

Worrying I have walked too far upon the lake, I give up and drive to Painted Rock.

iv

The man in black clothes lies crumpled on his stomach. He feels my approach because my feet no longer break through the salt. He senses my vibrations.

He rises to his knees. I touch his shoulder beneath the too-soon twilight.

His hand touches the stiffening hair above my neck. And I bend over to kiss his salt-crusted head.

v

Our return from Soda Lake is not through the same footprints that I remember.

From the distance of the sky, the two of us waver into one. A supreme passing into oneself, he thinks, beneath the Earth's diminishing light.

Stepping onto the shore, he pauses to gaze upward, toward the top of the hill where a man stands by his car staring down at him. He believes the man is lost after disappearing into the white salt lake.

He watches until the man on the hill fritters away into the last remnants of the straw-colored sky, and there is only one. And He is there.

ACKNOWLEDGMENTS

My deep gratitude to Kevin Clark and David Hull for seeing into the mysteries of *Soda Lake* from early on, and to Armando Marino for his visionary painting on the front cover. To my publisher Tyson Cornell for his profound belief in *Soda Lake*, and to Hailie Johnson for her guidance shaping the text and Kellie Kreiss for her clear-eyed editing. To Brad Campbell for his uncanny insights into McCuade and urging my journey to Donegal to find him. To Jim Muto, for his inspiration going back decades...to Paris and Pont Authou. For the timely assistance from Robin Miura and Harry Kirchner, and to Mary Kay Harrington, Glenn Irvin, Ginger Hendrix, and Al Landwehr for their crucial help with the early drafts of *Soda Lake*. To Jonny White for his mystical apprehension of the book, and to my faithful reader—John Harrington. Thanks to the Antioch Review and The Alaska Quarterly for publishing excerpts from *Soda Lake*, and to the Heinrich Boll Foundation for supporting me with a residency at the Boll Cottage on Achill Island. Finally, to my daughter Maya for helping me to understand, and to my love, Amanda, for her constant faith and encouragement.